This couldn't

Apart from her _____ was remotely famili_____ her. Gone was her sh_____, and in its place a long, glossy, caramel-brown ponytail swept across her shoulders in a caress of curls. Her face, which _____ seemed slightly too long for her, w_____ full. In fact all of her was _____ hite sundress fell from dec_____, flowing across voluptuous breasts before cas_____ding over a high and round _____swirling against the enticing tilt of her _____ curvaceous behind and firm thighs. She seemed taller, more sure of herself, and a secret smile played about her lips as if she knew things that others could never understand.

A thundering wave of pure sexual energy rode off her, spinning him into its orbit and rolling him inside its core. His groin tightened as a wondrous hot bolt of anticipation and excitement pounded through him. A second later his brain caught up with his body, its reaction horrified and stunned.

This is _____ We made _____

'You— _____ ord and he _____

Dear Reader

Christmas in Australia is a few days after the summer equinox, and it's the start of a traditional two-week holiday. Families flock to the coast to camp, rent holiday houses, or to be spoiled in boutique hotels, and the 'No Vacancy' signs glow red until well into January. In my state of Victoria, the Bellarine Peninsula, with its fabulous wineries, gourmet cafés and restaurants and quiet bayside beaches, is a popular destination—as is the nearby Surf Coast on the Great Ocean Road. With its rugged coastline and the Otway rainforest behind it, it's the perfect combination of forest and beach. If you want to holiday at either of these places you have to book a year in advance, as many families have been camping down there for sixty years or more.

It's family time. It's fun traditions—like decorating the tree, the annual beach cricket match, playing charades and board games, reading and teaching kids how to surf. Some people get really enthusiastic, and entire families enter the many 'open water' swims and beach runs, but no matter their energy levels everyone uses the time to kick back from routine and to recharge the batteries for another year ahead.

Despite being opposites, Hamish and Georgie have been best friends since university. They've been there for each other through good times and bad, so when Georgie asks Hamish one of the biggest favours a friend can ever ask he reluctantly agrees. He has one caveat: his family can never know.

Both Georgie and Hamish have totally different plans for Christmas, but the universe has a different idea again. Hamish finds himself living his worst nightmare. He's in the heart of his extended family at Christmas, and Georgie and their secret are there too.

I hope you enjoy spending Christmas at Weeroona with the Pettigrew family. For pictures of the beautiful Bellarine Peninsula and Surf Coast head to my website at www.fionalowe.com. You can also find me on Facebook and Twitter.

Wishing all my readers a very Merry Christmas and a New Year filled with reading.

Fiona x

NEWBORN BABY FOR CHRISTMAS

BY
FIONA LOWE

First published in Great Britain 2012
by Mills & Boon, an imprint of Harlequin (UK) Limited.
Harlequin (UK) Limited, Eton House,
18-24 Paradise Road, Richmond, Surrey TW9 1SR

© Fiona Lowe 2012

ISBN: 978 0 263 89208 6

Harlequin (UK) policy is to use papers that are natural, renewable and recyclable products and made from wood grown in sustainable forests. The logging and manufacturing process conform to the legal environmental regulations of the country of origin.

Printed and bound in Spain
by Blackprint CPI, Barcelona

Always an avid reader, **Fiona Lowe** decided to combine her love of romance with her interest in all things medical, so writing Medical Romance™ was an obvious choice! She lives in a seaside town in southern Australia, where she juggles writing, reading, working and raising two gorgeous sons with the support of her own real-life hero!

Recent books by the same author:

LETTING GO WITH DR RODRIGUEZ
SYDNEY HARBOUR HOSPITAL: TOM'S REDEMPTION*
CAREER GIRL IN THE COUNTRY
SINGLE DAD'S TRIPLE TROUBLE
THE MOST MAGICAL GIFT OF ALL
HER BROODING ITALIAN SURGEON
MIRACLE: TWIN BABIES

Sydney Harbour Hospital

**These books are also available in eBook format
from www.millsandboon.co.uk**

For Joanne, with special thanks for all your help
regarding the practical and legal issues surrounding AI.

CHAPTER ONE

Nine years ago

'LONDON via Africa?'

Dr Georgina Lambert high-fived her best mate, Hamish, and stomped on the eddies of disappointment that threatened to churn her stomach. 'That's awesome news.'

They'd just finished a fabulous hour of surfing and she quickly unwrapped the bulging white paper parcel of fish and chips that sat between them on a beach towel. Better to do that than think about the fact Hamish would soon be leaving Australia. Leaving her.

Breathing in the addictive aroma of salt and fat to block out her sadness, she said, 'I guess this means we're all grown up now.'

Hamish grinned as he brushed his wet, sun-and-salt-bleached curls out of his twinkling cornflower-blue eyes. 'Grown up? Never.'

And that was Hamish to a T. He was the Pied Piper of fun and good times and generous in his inclusion of all. From the moment she'd met him when he'd dragged her out of her college study at university and had taken her to his then girlfriend's party, he'd been telling her she needed to 'take chances and live a little.' Numerous girlfriends, a hundred parties later, along with a tough and gruelling study load, they were best friends.

They had the sort of friendship that grew from sharing life-altering experiences. Both of them understood the fine line between life and death that most people outside medicine had no clue about.

They knew they could talk to each other about things that would instantly kill a conversation at a cocktail party, and yet they understood that sometimes silence and just being there was all that was required. They made each other laugh and there'd been the odd time when they'd even cried together.

Over the years they'd leaned on each other at different times and Georgina couldn't imagine her life without him.

Returning his smile with an affectionate shake of her head, she said, 'Come to think of it, growing up would be your worst nightmare, wouldn't it?'

He laughed. 'Absolutely. Fortunately, big brothers Ben and Caleb are doing all the responsible stuff, and that has to be enough for the Pettigrew parents.'

She raised a brow because despite his party-boy ways, Hamish was a talented and reliable doctor. 'Not to mention six years of medical school, three years of internship and now a job in A and E at St Thomas's, London.'

He popped the ring pull on his can of drink. 'It's given me some parent cred for sure, and thankfully Ben's impending fatherhood has distracted them beautifully from the "when are you going to settle down?" question.'

Seagulls squawked around them, ever hopeful of getting some of the fish that nestled next to crisp and golden chips. She tore off a strip of white paper, wrapping it around the steaming-hot battered fish.

'I didn't know you were going to be an uncle.' Deep down inside her the hope that one day she'd be a mother flared, as it always did at the mention of a baby. 'London means you'll miss the birth of your first nephew or niece.'

'It's no biggie. Caleb will take his uncle duties seriously enough for both of us.' He shrugged. 'I'll post the kid a Paddington Bear from London.'

And there it was—the reason they were best friends and not lovers. They both wanted vastly different things out of life. A vague sadness stirred—one that always moved inside her whenever she thought about the fact he didn't want a family. Not that she thought everyone should have kids; she didn't. She accepted people's life choices, but Hamish had so much to give and he was really good with young patients.

Despite their close friendship and years of working together, and despite having tried a hundred different questions to try and find out why he was so adamant about staying single and not having children, she was no closer to knowing. She didn't understand his stance at all.

But adamant he was. There was a certain universal irony that a man so easy on the eyes, so genetically perfect that women stopped and stared while their subconscious said, *Good genes for baby making*, wasn't interested in becoming a father. Over the years, she'd watched as women had unwittingly flocked to him, investing too much of themselves too fast until it was too late. When Hamish dated a woman he was hers exclusively until the day he ended it, and 'ending it' happened frequently.

Perhaps because of his lack of commitment and the fact she wasn't interested in short-term relationships, there'd always been this unspoken rule between them that nothing would ever jeopardise their friendship.

That and chemistry. Or to be precise, a lack of it on Hamish's side, with the exception of one drunk moment that had stopped almost before it had started. He'd only ever treated her like a buddy and over the years she'd realised why. Every girlfriend he'd ever had was a certain body type—tall, willowy and perfect.

With her short waist, solid legs and wide hips, she was

so far removed from willowy it was a joke. Although initially she may have hoped for more than friendship from him, she'd soon realised friendship was what they did best and she treasured it.

They were mates, at ease with each other and very well aware of each other's foibles.

Munching in companionable silence, their hungry mouths devoured the wickedly wonderful salt- and fat-laden feast until all that was left was greasy paper.

Hamish wiped his mouth and asked, 'What about you, Georgie? You and Jonas going to open a family practice with a white picket fence and have a team of rug rats?'

Her bruised and battered heart limped in her chest and she delayed her answer momentarily by taking a slug of her drink. 'About me and Jonas…'

Hamish's gaze scanned her face, his eyes full of worry. 'What?'

This time she shrugged and tried to keep her voice steady. 'Not happening.'

His hand shot out and pressed hers. 'Hell, since when?'

'Since last week. He's going to Sydney to do orthopaedics and his change of plans includes changing girlfriends.'

His eyes darkened. 'I never liked the bastard.'

She hiccoughed, appreciating his support. 'You say that every time I get dumped.'

He squeezed her hand and let it go. 'Yeah, well, that's what friends are for and remember, there've been times when you've done the dumping.'

'True, only this time I thought he was the one.'

He shook his head so hard that salt water sprayed her. 'For God's sake, Georgie, why do you always do this? You're only twenty-six and you've got loads of time to land the guy who wants nothing more than to make babies with you.'

Only she wasn't so sure. Unlike Hamish, she didn't have prospective partners lining up around the block and she knew from experience she didn't attract men from the first signal. She was more of a 'personality' girl than one with stunning good looks.

She thought about how he often talked about his brothers and their enthusiasm for settling down. 'Ben and Caleb sound perfect. It's a shame you don't have another brother for me.' She ate more chips. 'Got any cousins?'

He shot her his cheeky trademark grin. 'Only Richard, and he's less likely to settle down than me.'

'Wow, that's really saying something,' she teased.

'Poor George. You met the wrong Pettigrew.' His grin slowly transformed into something more serious. 'Stop worrying about settling down and just get out there and live your life. If you're still single at thirty-five *then* you've got something to stress about.'

An image from a movie she'd seen recently flipped into her head. She grinned. 'Is this where we make a pact to marry each other at thirty-five if we're both still single?'

'God, no.' A horrified expression ripped across his face, leaving her in no doubt about his feelings. 'You know I don't want any of that stuff. I want adventure, excitement, fun and good times. And surfing with you.'

She gave him a wry smile and stomped on the crazy sort of sadness that was still lingering from when he'd blithely thought nothing of missing the birth of his niece or nephew. 'Surfing with me is going to be a bit tricky from London.'

Saying it made it real, and tears built behind her eyes. Her best friend, the one person who always championed her, was leaving to cross the world. 'What am I going to do without you around the corner to whinge and moan to after a crappy day, laugh with, surf with and generally fail to solve the world's problems with over wine?'

He leaned forward, his blue eyes filled with sincerity. 'No matter where I am, if you need me, I'm only a phone call away.'

She took in a big, deep, breath and mustered a smile because, no matter how much she would miss him, she wanted him happy and she knew this adventure was what he wanted. 'Same back atcha, mate. Go slay England.'

He gave her a wink. 'That's what I'm planning.'

One year ago

'Okay, girl, here goes,' Georgie muttered to herself as she stood on the veranda of Hamish's beautifully restored California bungalow. The hot afternoon December sun beat in, heating the earthy brown and yellow mosaic tiles, which warmed the soles of her feet through thin sandals. Raising her index finger, she firmly pressed the recessed copper doorbell while her stomach sprang cartwheels. As the brisk ring faded away, her ears strained for familiar firm footsteps.

You should have texted him first.

She turned away from the door, wanting to run back to her car and take off at top speed.

Stop it. Surprising each other is what we do. Stick to the plan, it's now or never.

She spun back, staring intently at the familiar art nouveau leadlight in the front door as if it was going to offer her peace of mind. She sucked in a deep breath.

The door swung open. 'Georgie!'

His malt-whisky voice—filled with deep surprise and absolute delight—flowed smoothly around her. Before she could squeak out a 'Hi', Hamish stepped forward, wrapped his arms firmly around her in a bear hug and lifted her off the ground. Swinging her around easily, he did two complete turns before setting her down again.

Twinkling eyes stared down at her. 'God, it's good to see you.'

She caught her breath. 'And you.'

He hugged her again. 'Come in. Come in.'

He ushered her into the house, leading the way down a central corridor until they stood in the light and airy extension. He kept his gaze glued on her. 'I can't believe it's you. I thought you were in Perth?'

Although they'd traded emails and texts, six months had flashed past since she'd last seen him and she found herself staring at him, not quite able to fill the well. His hair covered a little less of his forehead than it used to and a shorter style had taken out a lot of the curls. He had more laughter lines around his eyes but other than that he looked the same—tall, toned, sun kissed and radiating enthusiasm for life.

After five years in London and Africa—where she'd visited him twice—he'd returned to Australia and bought this house on a tree-lined street in Geelong. It was close to his beloved coast and only a couple of hours' drive from his parents.

Not that he'd settled down. He spent at least three months of the year away with Giving Back, spearheading groups of doctors for the charity and working in developing countries.

He was very generous in his permanent offer for her to use the house for mini-breaks from Melbourne any time she wished. She'd envisaged using it often but at his housewarming party everything had changed when she'd met Luke. 'Lovely Luke', as all her friends called him, and she'd agreed, happily following him to Perth. The nickname had stuck right up until three months ago.

'I'm back and working in Melbourne.' She smiled at him, hoping he didn't spot the tension that coiled through her like a preloaded spring. Her heart galloped like a racehorse and her stomach swished back and forth like a washing machine. It took everything she had to work at making herself sound normal—the absolute opposite of how she was feeling because everything hung on his answer to a question.

'I thought *you* were in Peru until February. In fact, I didn't believe Joel Goldsmith when he told me you were back.'

He grimaced. 'Sorry, George, I know we usually let each other know when we're in or out of the country but things have been a bit crazy. Dad had a myocardial infarction so I came home early.'

'Oh, God.' Georgie had only met Hamish's parents a few times—at graduation, briefly in London and once at a charity dinner for Giving Back, but that didn't lessen her concern. 'Is he okay?'

Hamish nodded. 'He was lucky. They were in town doing Christmas shopping and ordering supplies for the guesthouse when it happened, so he went straight to the hospital and they inserted a stent. He's doing great. In fact, he's fitter now than before it all happened.'

'That's good to hear.' Georgie automatically swung round at the sound of footsteps.

A woman who looked to be in her early twenties, complete with bedroom eyes and a boyish figure which was barely covered by a skimpy bikini, appeared barefoot at the French doors. Absolutely nothing about her sagged or bulged—her youth guaranteeing everything held itself up on its own and stayed in its rightful place. She was perfect in every way and she'd probably never met a stretch mark or a full support bra, let alone sculpted underwear.

Georgie's insides slumped and she suddenly felt all of her thirty-four years. This woman—

She's a girl.

This girl was the ideal example of Hamish's preferred type—everything perfectly proportioned and nothing over or undersized in any way.

Everything I'm not.

Over the years she'd got skilled at hiding the way each new girlfriend made her feel, so she tilted her head and raised her brows as if to say, *Nothing's changed, I see*.

Hamish caught the look and winked. 'Stephanie, this is my very good friend, Georgina.'

Although Hamish invariably shortened her name to Georgie or George, he always introduced her by her full name. It was at odds with his easygoing manner and she often wondered why he didn't feel other people should treat her name with the same casual familiarity he always did.

'Hi, Stephanie. Good to meet you.' She gave her a friendly wave, similar to the ones she'd given to the many girlfriends of Hamish's over the years. Girlfriends who'd once been of similar age but were now a lot younger.

Well, she was the grown-up in the room so she planned to be the one in charge. Keeping her gaze on Stephanie's face, she said, 'I just have some business to discuss with Hamish and then he's all yours again. I promise I won't keep him too long.'

Stephanie looked straight at Hamish, managing to combine equal amounts of a disappointed pout with a provocative glance that together said, *I'm holding you to that.* 'I guess I'll wait out by the pool, then.'

When Hamish didn't disagree, Stephanie turned and disappeared from view.

'We have *business* to discuss?' Hamish's furrowed brow matched the rest of his confused expression.

She bit her lip. *This is it.* This was the reason she'd come. The moment she'd been working towards for three long months. She'd expected to have more time, but everything had suddenly been brought forward by his early arrival home and her disquiet that he might disappear again just as quickly. As each year passed Hamish seemed to travel more and more with Giving Back.

I really could wait.

No, you can't. Tick tock, tick tock. There's no time like the present.

Gripping her bag close to her side, she heard the crackle of squished legal papers scrunching inside it. 'Can we go into your office so we're not interrupted?'

Hamish startled—his eyes suddenly wide and his face pinched. 'Hell, George, what's going on?'

Everything she wanted came down to this yet-to-be-had conversation—the one she'd practised in front of her cheval mirror so many times she could recite it in her sleep. She swallowed and hooked his gaze. 'Do you remember just before you went to London, you said to me that that if I ever needed you, I just had to ask?'

Hamish's blood chilled as his gut gave a sickening lurch. Georgie had *never* asked him for anything before and his brain shot straight to disaster. He covertly studied her, searching for the cachectic look of cancer.

Nothing.

She stood before him with her short-cropped brown hair mussed and looking as she always did—slightly dishevelled and as if she'd thrown on whatever clothes had landed at the end of her bed over the previous week.

A smooth expanse of olive skin broken only by the shimmering of a jewelled navel ring separated the top of a pair of baggy happy pants and a white embroidered blouse, which she'd tied under her breasts. Breasts he'd always admired despite the fact they were slightly too big for the rest of her body. Georgie always hated it that her body was wrongly proportioned and he knew she spent a lot of time at the gym trying to dominate it into submission, but without much success.

But all of that aside and taking into account her usual aura of general uncertainty about the world she lived in, she looked fit and healthy and not remotely sick.

The fact she wanted privacy scared him and he quickly ushered her through to the office, his mind racing, trying to preempt her question but coming up blank. 'Of course I remember.'

'Good.' She chewed her thumbnail the way she always did when she was nervous.

His anxiety ratcheted up a few more notches as her eyes

flickered with a myriad of emotions, but he could only recognise fear backed up by determination. Surely knowing had
to be better than this agony. 'Spit it out, George.'

Her shoulders squared and she shot him a tight smile that
combined a flare of hope tied up with despair. 'I want your
sperm.'

CHAPTER TWO

'EXCUSE me?' Hamish tugged at his ear, certain he must have misheard.

'I want a baby, Haim. I want you to be the father.'

His building anxiety exploded, sending his blood swooping to his feet and making his head spin. The crushing weight of unease pressed down so hard on his chest that it made breathing difficult. Of all the things he'd anticipated her asking, this wasn't one of them.

He half fell onto his chair, sending it skating backwards. 'What the...? Georgie, I don't want to be a father.'

Her mouth flattened on one side. 'I know you don't and I'm not asking you to be one.'

He shook his head, trying to quieten the white noise so he could make sense of what she was saying. 'You just said you want me to be the father of your baby.'

She wrung her hands. 'I know. Sorry. This isn't coming out right.'

'Damn right it isn't.' His tight throat and dry mouth barely allowed words to be formed. 'You and Luke should be having this conversation, not you and me.'

'Luke's in Perth. We split up three months ago.' The words fell flat as her breasts rose and fell. 'He doesn't want to be a father.'

'Neither do I,' he heard himself yell.

She sat down and pulled her chair up to the desk so she was opposite him and she leaned in close. Yearning burned so brightly in her eyes that he squinted.

'Although it's a shock to you, Haim, I've had time to think about this and to argue out every single pro and con. This isn't a whim. Please hear me out.'

Her entreaty penetrated his shock and a sigh rolled through him. What harm was there in listening?

Plenty.

But he couldn't get past that desolate look in her eyes. 'Shoot.'

She gave a brisk nod of thanks and sat back on her chair, all businesslike and professional. 'It's no secret that I've always wanted a family. Growing up an only child is…quiet. Lonely. When Mum and Dad died…' She bit her lip and breathed in deeply. 'Since they died two years ago, it's like I have this empty space inside me, constantly reminding me I'm alone. I thought when Luke suggested we buy a house in Perth it meant we were moving forward as a couple into the future. A future with children, a family.'

Her voice wobbled for a moment. 'But I was wrong. The moment I brought up the idea of children, Luke bolted and the relationship crashed and burned.'

Hamish totally related to the running but he wasn't fool enough to say so. All he knew was that when a woman he was dating started pointing to strollers in the street, he was out the door faster than an athlete on steroids.

Georgie's fingers drummed on the polished oak of his desk, her agitation palpable. 'My biological clock isn't just ticking, it's on full scream continuous alarm. I'm running out of time. In three days I'm turning thirty-five,' her voice cracked and rose. 'Thirty-five, Hamish. The age you told me it was okay to panic.'

An accusatory finger pointed at him, bringing back his off-the-cuff comment from so long ago to haunt him like a tormented ghost. How easy it was to spout words—they evaporated long before the mark they left started to fade.

Her intensity had his heart pounding as tendrils of unease threatened to coalesce into fear. It was time to put perspective back into the conversation.

'So all of this is because of your birthday?' He tried a reassuring smile. 'Come on, Georgie, you know I knew nothing at twenty-six. I was just talking through my hat and thirty-five was a random number I plucked out of the air to cheer you up at the time. You and I both know that thirty-five isn't old.'

She jerked in her seat as if he'd just fired a bullet through her and her mouth hardened. 'You remember Sue Lipton?'

Hamish nodded, wondering why someone they hadn't seen in years was being brought into the conversation. 'Sure, didn't she do anaesthetics?'

'Yes, and she married Ryan Spedding. They're on the IVF programme.' She pressed her forefinger of her right hand against the thumb of her left, numbering off. 'So are Emily and Lewis Pearce, and Jessica James has been trying to get pregnant for eleven months.'

He rubbed his forehead as an ache started behind his eyes. 'And you're telling me this why?'

'Because they're *our* age and they're having problems. You're a doctor, Hamish, and you know that every single day that passes reduces my fertility just that little bit more. I don't have any more time to waste. If I want a family of my own I have to get pregnant now.'

'I know you've always loved the drama of life but now you need perspective.' He heard his voice—the tone he used to soothe distressed patients. 'You do have time to meet someone else.'

'Stop and listen to yourself, Hamish.' Her arm shot out for emphasis. 'You're the perfect example of the men out there running from commitment. I respect your choice but because you and so many other men are making it, we both know my chances of meeting someone who wants marriage and a family are not remotely good betting odds.'

She folded her hands in her lap as if she was searching for calmness, and when she spoke her voice was softer. 'So I'm bypassing that step. I have a good job, I'm financially secure, sadly thanks to Mum and Dad's deaths I can buy a house outright and I want a baby. I want my *own* family, Haim, and if I have to do it on my own then so be it.'

Her abject frustration and disillusionment bounced between them. He'd never wanted a child but Georgie had longed for one for almost as long as he'd known her. That fact didn't lessen the reality that her request of him was too much to ask.

'I get it. You want a kid and you're skipping the relationship part to get one. So use an anonymous donor.'

She chewed her lip. 'I could, but...'

Every part of him yelled, *Stay firm, don't ask*, but she looked so forlorn that he heard himself saying, 'But what?'

She leaned toward him again, her face earnest and bright and willing him to understand. 'A donor's bio of height, weight, eye, hair colour and job doesn't tell me personality and that's not reassuring. You're my best friend and I know you, warts and all. Despite your love of a party, you're great stock with a sturdy gene pool.'

'You make me sound like a racehorse,' he spluttered as effrontery swirled around the ego-warming compliment that she wanted her child to have his genes.

She shot him a wry smile. 'You're intelligent, healthy, giving and most importantly not a psychopath. I want my child to have the smarts to deal with life.'

He spun in the chair, trying to cache his thoughts so he could separate them from the abject terror that thundered through his veins at the thought of a child. 'I've spent years making sure I didn't create a little Hamish and now you want me to do it deliberately? Aren't you worried you might be adding another male to the world who isn't interested in playing happy families?'

She rolled her eyes. 'I might be adding a girl or perhaps a boy like your brothers or a throwback to your dad. As a father of three sons he obviously had no concerns about being a father.'

Four sons. But he didn't correct her because he'd never told her about Aaron. Once he'd left his home town of Jindi River to go to university, he'd never mentioned his beloved younger brother to anyone—not even Georgie. It was so much easier that way.

She unzipped her massive handbag and pulled out some printed pages bound with green tape and laid them on the table between them. 'I've thought long and hard about this, Hamish, and I want to reassure you that all I want is your sperm. Not you, not your time or your money. This will be *my* baby.'

A niggle of concern jabbed him under his ribs. 'And when the kid asks about his father?'

Her mouth firmed with resolve. 'I'll tell him or her that I used a donor.'

He studied her closely, trying to work out if her words really matched her beliefs. 'So, you don't even expect me to be Uncle Hamish?'

She laughed—a spurt of disbelieving sound. 'Do you even know how to be an uncle? I'm not sure your nephews know you very well, do they?'

He tried to feel insulted but failed because she was right. No matter how much he might want to argue with her on that point, the fact was he didn't see his five nephews very often at all. They were good kids and he sent them birthday gifts and happily enjoyed their company at Christmas, but that was enough. He was the *fun* uncle and if he didn't see much of them then he couldn't let them down like he'd let down Aaron.

He couldn't risk having his own child and repeating past mistakes.

He tried to head off this crazy request by going straight to the heart of the matter. 'Georgie, something like this could ruin our friendship.'

Her straight-shooting gaze hooked him, filled with honesty. 'It won't. Another reason I'm asking you is because I know you don't want a child.'

He had a moment of feeling like he was fighting quicksand. 'I don't understand how me not wanting a child makes you ask me.'

'You'll leave me in peace to raise him or her alone and do things my way. This is *my* baby, my new-start family.'

He stared at her as if she were a stranger. Georgie had always wanted the happy-ever-after and the white picket fence so very, very much that he couldn't believe she was abandoning it completely. 'Are you really sure you want to do this all on your own? You always said—'

'That's the past.' Her plump lips compressed as her jaw tightened. 'I want my own family again, to feel part of something. Connected.'

The quiver in her voice socked him straight in the heart. Supporting Georgie through the funeral of her parents had been one of the hardest things he'd ever had to do. He had relatives coming out of his ears but Georgie didn't.

Her shoulders rose and fell. 'Hey, I know it's not perfect, but what in life is? The baby and I will be a team of two, and you know what? It's okay because the flip side is that I get to make all the decisions. I have control and so there's no risk of me and the baby being abandoned when a man decides yet again that I'm not enough for him.'

He saw the facts on her face and in the depths of her eyes matching up with her words. She was deadly serious. He knew she'd always liked to try and control things in her life and not take too many risks, but having a baby? *Hell.* He ran his hands through his hair. Having a baby was *the* biggest out-of-control step in life a person could take.

A long-ago image of Aaron on his bike and he himself screaming 'Stop!' rose in his head like a spectre—a haunting ghost who refused to be completely silenced. No matter how many years he'd worked as a doctor, saving lives, travelling to developing countries to help improve the lives of others, the pain of losing a brother had become as much a part of him as his own gristle and bone.

He tried to breathe but it was like trying to move his chest against circular bands of steel. He had to tell her he couldn't do this and he would, the moment he could get the words out.

'Haim, I realise I've shocked you and my request is totally out of the blue for you.' She pushed the paperwork towards him and leaned in. 'But for me it's a long-held dream. A child will make my life more worthwhile and give me family again. I want a baby so badly that my arms and heart ache constantly.'

He was intimate with heartache and the throb of a faded despair that never fully went away. A baby would make him revisit a maelstrom of emotions and he refused to go there. 'I'm sorry, Georgie… I don't think I can help you.'

Her shoulders slumped for a moment and then her chocolate-brown eyes hooked his gaze, filled with everything they'd ever shared. 'I've never asked you for anything, Hamish, and I never will again, but right now I'm asking you, my closest friend in the whole world, not to make a hasty decision, not to say *yes* or *no*. All I'm asking is that you think about it. Sleep on it and tell me tomorrow or in three days.'

'It's not going—'

'It might. Time to think is always good. Please, Hamish. Take the papers, read them, write down all your questions and call me.' She slid her hand over his, her expression filled with pleading. 'We've always talked and shared everything.'

Not quite everything. He swallowed against a constricted

throat. God, he hadn't thought about Aaron in such a long time and today he was present in every sentence.

Tell her you can't be a sperm donor. Tell her it's an unequivocal no.

But her longing and despair swirled all around him, pulling at him in ways that made him hesitate.

'Hamish?'

Her voice sounded small and uncertain, reminding him of the weeks after her parents had died, and he found himself saying, 'I can't promise you anything, George, except I'll read the papers.'

'Thank you.' She rose to her feet and hugged him—her arms wrapping around him more tightly than usual.

Her breasts pressed against his chest and her fresh scent of summer flowers swirled around him, and for a split second his off-kilter world steadied. Then she stepped back and life went back to whatever could be called normal.

Hamish put a pouting Stephanie into a taxi and after a distracted goodbye kiss he headed back inside and poured himself a large glass of merlot. As he sat in his study and opened the legal document that Georgie had left him, he hoped he'd find the clause that would provide the perfect excuse for him to say an absolute and indisputable *no* to her request that he give her a baby.

God, he'd wanted to say *no*, but every time he'd tried, it had been like being in a fight and having two guys grab hold of his arms to prevent him from taking a swing. He'd opened his mouth but the look on her face when she'd talked about not having a family had stopped him dead. It shouldn't have because this was as much about him as it was about her, and he knew exactly why he should say *no*.

He'd failed to keep Aaron safe, failed miserably at being a big brother, and wasn't that the training ground for fatherhood? He couldn't be responsible for a child.

So tell her that.

But that would involve telling her about his little brother, about the day that was etched into his mind like a tattoo. He wasn't prepared to do that. He'd found a way to live with his guilt and resurrecting the past had no value at all. Besides, Georgie wasn't asking him to be a hands-on father. She'd been very clear on that. He'd be a donor known only to her and with no connection to the baby other than his donated DNA.

Could he do that? He stared out the window. He knew men who prided themselves on being sperm donors and didn't seem to give a moment's thought to the fact that they were creating a child—a human being who one day might knock on their door, wanting to connect. Hell, he didn't want that to happen. He wasn't father material and he wasn't letting another child down. He knew the catastrophic consequences of that.

He took a slug of wine, wishing Georgie had never asked him such a huge favour and yet he knew and understood exactly why she had.

What had started out all those years ago as him encouraging 'the quiet girl' at college to get involved had unexpectedly turned into a special friendship that had got them both through the tough life of being a med student, the fraught life of an intern and had survived both of them taking slightly different paths in medicine. Not to mention weathering their relationships with other people. Their bond was stronger than superglue and he'd stopped counting how often she'd randomly called him just at a time when he'd needed some support.

Georgie was the antithesis of him. He'd act first, think second. She'd weigh up the pros and cons, which was a great strategy for a doctor but not when it was a movie or a quick meal choice, but once she committed to something she gave it her all. He loved that about her. She'd put herself out of her comfort zone more than once, hiking the overland track in Tasmania with him and learning to surf. Throughout the years they'd always been there for each other, although up until now they'd never really tested the promise they'd made nine years ago.

No matter where I am, if you need me, I'm only a phone call away. He'd made that offer to her in good faith and believing in it utterly.

Son, never make a promise you don't intend to keep.

He gave an ironic groan. He was pretty sure his father hadn't been thinking about sharing genes when he'd hammered that lesson into him between the ages of five and twenty. Not even the thought of sex was enough to allay his anxiety. Not that he was against the idea of sex with Georgie. He'd never pursued it because their friendship had always come first and he'd never wanted to risk losing it, but, hell, he was male and there'd been times when he'd wondered what it would be like to bury his head in those amazing breasts. The night they'd graduated he'd got close and then common sense had made them both jump away from each other with an embarrassed laugh, both agreeing that it was a bad idea generated by too much champagne.

He rubbed his face with his hands, feeling the rasp of stubble against his palms. If he applied logic to the problem and removed the emotions, it came down to a single fact. His best friend, a woman who would do anything for him, needed his help. Help he'd offered in the past. Help he was honour-bound to provide.

But where was the line drawn on the statute of reasonable friendship requests?

As much as he was concerned about the impact that him saying *yes* would have on their friendship, he was more worried about the impact of saying, *no.*

Georgie held her breath as she sat opposite Hamish in a quiet café overlooking the bay. It had been thirty hours since she'd asked him to be a sperm donor and she'd almost become obsessive compulsive in that time, constantly checking her phone. Last night as she'd sat curled up on the couch—there'd been no point going to bed because sleep had been beyond her—she'd lurched between *He agreed to read the paperwork, which means he's considering it and will say yes*, and the more resounding, *He'll say no*.

The fact he'd finally called her and said, 'I need to ask you some questions,' had fired hope into her, but it was now tinged with dread as she watched Hamish's clear and steady gaze move over the printed words. Her heart bounced against her ribs and the sound echoed in her ears, deafening her.

Was it too much to ask of him?

Maybe. No. It had never occurred to her *not* to ask him. He was her best friend and it made total sense to her that he would be the sperm donor for her child. He had great genes, a caring nature and for reasons he'd never really elucidated, despite some gentle probing over the years, he didn't want to be a father.

She, on the other hand, wanted a baby so much it hurt. She was an experienced doctor, enjoyed family medicine and had been told hundreds of times she was great with kids so she knew she could do this parenting gig on her own and not involve him at all. It was a win-win situation all round.

Hamish glanced up from the second page of the document with a familiar wicked gleam in his eyes that she hadn't seen since she'd floored him with her request. 'So, no sex?'

Her usually deep laugh sounded high-pitched and nervous.

She'd be lying to herself if she said she'd never fantasised about what sex would be like with Hamish. What woman wouldn't when faced with six feet two of a toned, tanned and buff surfer-fit body? But that had been a long time ago and she'd never been one for casual sex, especially if it risked their friendship.

'Sex is too random and this is too important to leave to

chance. I want the back-up of science and technology to maximise my chances of getting pregnant quickly. I'll have ultrasounds, and thirty-six hours before the intra-uterine insemination, I'll jab myself with follicle-stimulating hormone.'

His shoulders squared as they tightened with apprehension and his expression became serious once again. 'So I travel to the IVF clinic in Tasmania to make my deposits?'

'Yup. They have movies and magazines.' She tried to lighten his mood. 'That's the fun part for you.'

He rolled his eyes. 'Hardly, but we won't go there. Why Tasmania?'

'Privacy for both of us. The medical community here is too small and everyone knows everyone. Even if we went to Melbourne, we'd run into people from university. I'll pay for your air fares and your time because I don't want you embarrassed or compromised. I figured you could go down for a couple of weekends, enjoy a mini-break on the apple isle and bank a few deposits, so to speak.'

A grudging flash of admiration crossed his face. 'You've really thought this through.'

She twisted her hands in her lap. 'It's all I've been thinking about for months.'

Thinking, dreaming and planning.

He nodded slowly, his expression contemplative, and he returned to the document.

Time slowed down to a crawl and she wished she could dive inside his head and see and hear exactly what he was thinking. Instead, she had to sit and wait. She was so used to being in charge at work that it didn't sit easily.

'They'll freeze the sperm?'

'Yes.'

His gaze bored into her. 'And if you don't get pregnant from my donations, what then?'

She chewed on her lip. 'Would you be prepared to donate more?'

A long sigh rumbled out of him. 'To be honest, George, I'm not even certain I want to do it once.'

'Oh.' Her stomach sank as hope dribbled away. She now wished he'd just said *no* over the phone. She sat tracing the pool of condensation from her water that had dribbled down onto the tabletop.

Hamish leaned forward and stirred his coffee so hard that some splashed into the saucer. 'I won't have my name on the birth certificate,' he muttered softly, 'and I doubt you can get around that.'

His clipped words hammered her and she spoke quickly, leaping onto a spluttering kernel of hope, keen to allay his concerns. 'You won't be named. The one thing that Mum and Dad's deaths has given me is financial security. When I add in my income, even though it will be reduced with part-time work, I won't need to claim family assistance. That gives me a loophole to avoid naming the father and I promise that you won't be named.'

'What about us spending time together after the baby's born?'

'I…' God, why hadn't she thought of that? She'd emphasised that this baby was hers and only hers, and she believed that utterly. She shredded a paper napkin and tried to think, realising for the first time that a baby might change everything between them. 'I understand what you're saying. I guess I get a babysitter.' A heavy feeling gathered in her chest and she rubbed her sternum.

He ran one hand across the back of his neck as if his appeal against a death sentence had just been squashed and then he finally closed the document. '*If* I do this, I have a rule.'

If.

A squeal of excitement bubbled up in her as she sensed she was unexpectedly close to getting what she wanted. 'What is it?'

A seriously stern look entered his eyes, extinguishing the

usual fun that mostly lived there. The only other times she'd seen him like this had been when he'd had to deliver bad news to patients or their relatives. The bubbles of excitement inside her burst, splattering trepidation from tip to toe.

'Georgie, my parents must never find out. *Ever*.'

His words roared around her and she wasn't totally certain she understood. 'Your parents?'

He nodded stiffly. 'They can't know they have another grandchild. If they found out it would hurt them too much and I don't want to inflict that sort of pain on them. They'd also descend on me and then you.' His hand raked through his hair. 'And I can't be responsible for the consequences.'

Sheer relief made her laugh because this *so* wasn't a problem. 'Now who's being overdramatic? Haim, in all the years I've known you, I've met your family, what...?' She did a mental count. 'Three times, so this request is easily met. I'm in Melbourne and they're in Jindi River so we're hardly likely to run into each other. I'm making you a solemn promise that your parents will never find out about the baby.' She stared into his eyes, willing him to say *yes*.

He raised his outback-blue eyes to hers, meeting them full on, and deep down inside her something lurched. Confused and unsettled, she dropped her gaze and crossed her legs over the discombobulating sensation that spun there. 'You're a sperm donor. Nothing more and nothing less.'

Only for some odd reason she wasn't totally certain exactly who she was reassuring.

Silently, he picked up the pen she'd earlier placed on the table between them with a great deal of hope, and he drew off the lid very slowly. He pushed it onto the top of the pen before bringing the nib down towards the paper with an excruciating lack of speed, as if he still might stall and not sign.

She bit her lip so hard she tasted blood.

He paused with the pen a millimetre away from signing. 'It's a hell of a thing to ask, George.'

'I know.'

'If a child is born from this, it's totally your kid and nothing to do with me.'

'Absolutely. It's in the contract you're about to sign.'

Tension shot through his square jaw. 'If you do get pregnant, I don't want blow-by-blow updates or ultrasound pictures. I'm nothing more than a three-time donor.'

Three times? She wanted to argue that, ask for more, but she knew better. She'd take what she could get. 'I understand.'

'I don't want invitations to birthday parties either.'

'You're preaching to the converted.' A tiny whisper of concern gained volume. 'Haim, baby or no baby, we're still going to be friends, right?'

'I want to hope we can be.' He scrawled his name across the document.

Tears pricked her eyes. 'Thank you.'

Hamish didn't meet her gaze or reply. Instead, he downed his coffee in one long gulp.

Georgie picked up the legal papers, hugging them tightly to her chest, and sent up a heartfelt wish. Today was the first day of the rest of her life.

CHAPTER THREE

December

GEORGIE hummed 'Six White Boomers', the Christmas song about kangaroos pulling Santa's sleigh, and grinned. She'd been grinning almost non-stop for months, even during the five weeks when morning sickness had lasted all day, leaving her stomach inside out and the rest of her limp, like overcooked cabbage. During that time she'd existed almost exclusively on dry biscuits and ginger beer, and it would be a long time before she could face either of them again.

Even so, nothing could wipe the always-present smile off her face. She pressed her hand against her round belly, feeling a tiny foot under her palm, and pure delight made her laugh out loud. Despite the ultrasounds and her ever-increasing size, there were still moments when she couldn't quite believe she was pregnant. It had taken three cycles and three trips to Tasmania before she'd been given the news she'd craved for so long, and from the moment the pregnancy test had shown a definitive blue line, she'd treasured every second.

When she'd read the positive pregnancy test her first instinct had her reaching for the phone to ring Hamish and tell him the good news. Halfway through dialling she'd remembered his words.

If a child is born from this, it's totally your kid and nothing to do with me.

She'd abruptly dropped the phone. She couldn't believe she'd even thought to ring him because she'd been as adamant as he that this was *her* baby and not his in any way. No, Hamish needed to find out about the baby the exact same way as her other friends and colleagues—with a photo text when the baby was born.

The baby kicked, as if reminding her that sending those announcements wouldn't be too far away, and a fizz of excitement tingled through her. In a month's time—give or take two weeks—she'd finally hold her baby in her arms and right now she was in full-on nesting mode. It had taken longer than she'd thought to find a house to buy that suited her and her lease on her apartment had expired just as settlement had been finalised last week.

In most instances this would have been perfect timing with no need to find interim accommodation, but the house needed some renovations. Now she was technically living in her new home but surrounded by high stacks of cardboard boxes and the buzz of builders, carpenters, plumbers and cabinetmakers dragging the kitchen, bathroom and laundry into the twenty-first century. Painters roamed the rest of the house with their once-white but now paint-splattered dropsheets, freshening up the walls of the solid 1950s house with its spacious, light-filled rooms and large, decorative cornices. It was chaotic.

She'd called in during her lunch-break to speak with the building supervisor, but when she'd arrived Dennis had been on the phone so she'd left him to it and was waiting in the dining room, which was the only room currently free of the renovation frenzy.

Pulling open a box, she plucked out a small tabletop Christmas tree and placed it on the dropsheet-covered chiffonier. She knew it was silly to unpack it, let alone put it on display, given the total mess that surrounded her, but she'd always loved Christmas. Growing up, her parents had made it such a magical time and she was looking forward to re-creating that magic with her own child.

Despite feeling her parents' deaths keenly at this time of year and missing them like mad, she still loved the season and it seemed disrespectful not to have at least *one* sign of Christmas. She knew they'd have wanted her to keep their traditions going.

'Next year, Widget—' she'd used the affectionate term she'd been calling the baby from the moment she'd known she was pregnant '—this house will groan with decorations and you'll probably love the wrapping paper more than the presents.'

She desperately wanted to set up the nursery and she was actively practising patience while she waited for the deco-rators to finish. Meanwhile, the white cot and her amazing change table that would convert to a play table in the future were both still in their flat-pack state and her prize posses-sion—her mother's Amish rocking chair—was in the cor-ner of the dining room with a dustcover over it, waiting to be housed.

Dennis had assured her that everything would come to-gether in his promised time frame of two weeks, but given the chaos that didn't seem to be abating at all she was hav-ing trouble imagining the house finished in time. Meanwhile, she was showering at the practice and for evening meals she was working her way through the many restaurants that were part of her local shopping strip at the bottom of the street.

The whirr of a circular saw and the rhythmic banging of a hammer added their sound to the blaring radio that the trades-men always had playing, and Georgie decided that being at work was almost peaceful compared to this. Glancing at her watch, she realised her lunch-break was almost over and she hurried to find Dennis. As she entered the hall she heard a loud shout followed by an almighty crash and an emphatic stream of swearing.

Doubling back, she rushed towards the sound and arrived at the kitchen at the same moment as Dennis. He was swearing more loudly than his employees.

A white cloud of dust was settling around the young apprentice who lay sprawled and groaning on the floor surrounded by half of Georgie's ceiling. He was on his side with one leg lying at an odd angle. She instinctively looked up as if she'd forgotten the ten-foot height and needed to calculate the drop. 'Get my medical bag from my car. The silver four-wheel drive,' she shouted to no one in particular. 'My keys are on the hallstand seat.'

'On it.' One of the workmen hurriedly left the room, the loud thud of his workboots hitting the polished hall floorboards and reverberating back to her.

'I promised your mother I'd look after you, Mitch,' Dennis said, his face tinged with green. 'She's going to kill me.'

Clearing a space by swiping her foot back and forth through the debris, Georgie pulled her sundress over her legs for protection and knelt down next to the teenager.

'Mitch? Who am I?'

His face was twisted in pain. 'Sorry about your plaster, Dr Lambert.'

'Right now I'm more worried about you. That was quite a fall.' She looked at his pupils, which were thankfully the same size as each other. 'Did you hit your head? Black out?'

'I dunno. One minute I was on the beam and the next minute I was here.'

'Can you open and close your eyes for me?'

He looked at her as if she was slightly deranged but did as he was told, and Georgie was pleased to see his pupils reacting to light. She picked up his wrist, feeling for his pulse, and he yelped in pain. 'Sorry. You probably landed on this when you instinctively put it out to protect yourself. Sadly, we don't land as well as cats.'

Mitch moaned. 'Me hip's killing me.'

Reaching out her hand, she took his carotid pulse and counted for ten seconds. It was fast but relatively steady and she hoped the speed was due to pain and not internal bleeding. Only time would tell. 'Dennis, call an ambulance.'

The builder nodded, fishing his phone out of his overalls pocket and making the call.

Georgie examined Mitch's legs, which were bloody from cuts and scratches. One ankle was swelling before her eyes and his leg was rotated outwards, which wasn't a good sign. She added it to the growing list of injuries but possible fractures were the least of her concerns at the moment.

'Mitch, I need you to listen very carefully to me and only move when I tell you.'

The fear of getting into trouble morphed into a fear of a different kind and his entire body stiffened. Suddenly he looked a lot younger than his seventeen years. 'It hurts to move.'

'Good,' said Dennis. 'You won't be tempted to do any more stupid things.'

Despite the gruffly spoken words, Georgie could hear the worry and concern in the boss's voice and he had plenty to worry about. A fall like the one Mitch had just sustained meant a strong possibility of fractured vertebrae and a compromised spinal cord, along with a host of other injuries. 'Can you feel your fingers and toes?'

'Yeah.' He wiggled his fingers but flinched when he tried his toes. 'Me right leg feels wrong.'

At least he could feel it.

'Here's your bag, Doc.' Dennis knelt down opposite her and handed her the medical kit, which Greg, the carpenter, had just passed him.

'Thanks,' she called out to Greg. 'I need towels and sheets, please. They're in the linen press in the hall.'

'Sure thing.'

As he left the room, Georgie pulled the green whistle out of her bag—the emergency analgesia that patients sucked on for pain relief. 'Mitch, put this in your mouth and take deep breaths and it will help with the pain.'

The young man did as he was asked and Georgie started to assemble a cervical collar. 'I'm going to put this around your neck for support and then Dennis and I are going to roll you onto your back like you're a log. It might hurt.'

'That don't sound good.' Mitch's voice sounded small and scared.

'Sorry, mate, but until I know exactly what damage you've done to yourself, we're protecting your spine.' She started measuring for the collar, using an imaginary line from the top of his shoulder to where the collar would rest and then another from the chin. Putting as many of her fingers that fitted into the space, she used them to measure the distance.

A moment later with a series of clicks and clacks she adjusted the collar, using the locks, until it was the correct size. 'Dennis, I need you to hold Mitch's head like this.' She demonstrated.

'Can do.' Dennis's usually loud and beefy voice quavered slightly and his face had stayed white tinged with green. Despite that, he did exactly as he was asked, using his burly hands—one on each side of Mitch's cheeks—to keep his head in a neutral position.

Mitch wore a silver skull on a chain around his neck. 'I have to take this off,' she said, pulling back on the clasp, 'but I promise it will be safe.' She slipped it into her pocket and then slid the back portion of the collar behind his neck and folded the loop of Velcro inwards on top of the foam padding. After attaching it to the chinpiece, she tightened the collar,

using the tracheal hole as the anchor point. Mitch's chin pro-
truded over the collar, which was a good sign.

'Is it comfortable?'

'Yes. My neck never hurt. Just everything else.'

She needed to examine him fully but she wasn't prepared
to do that until she'd protected his spinal cord. She patted
his arm and said, 'Take another couple of deep breaths on
the green whistle.'

Greg had dropped onto the dusty floor two fluffy towels and her brand-new one-thousand-thread-count Egyptian
cotton sheets she'd bought to celebrate moving into her own
home. Linen she'd not even used yet.

She silenced her moan of disappointment as she rolled a
luxury towel and inserted it between Mitch's knees to keep
his legs apart and the head of both his femurs in their hip
sockets. Using one sheet, she tied his ankles together and
then wrapped another one around his hips. She'd stake her
bottom dollar he'd fractured his pelvis and, with the close
proximity of his bladder and bowel, that was a real concern.
'How are you travelling, Mitch?'

His eyes fluttered close to closing. 'This whistle's good
stuff.'

She gave a vote of thanks for Australian ingenuity and
inventions and smiled, having heard similar stories from
injured patients in the past. Mitch was going to need all the
help it could give him.

Glancing up at Dennis, she said, 'We need to move him
very carefully. You hold his ankles and support his legs and,
Greg, you put your hands on his hips and I'll take care of
his neck. On my count we're going to roll him very slowly
onto his back.'

She waited for the men to get into position. 'Mitch, are
you ready?'

'I guess.' He sounded hesitant and scared.

'Right, fellas. One, two, three.'

Mitch slowly came onto his back, his body in alignment, and the moment they took their hands away he sucked down another deep draft on the whistle.

'Great work, guys. Thanks.' Georgie rechecked Mitch's pulse and then took his blood pressure. Both were up. Was he bleeding?

She quickly primed an IV line by folding the plastic cord in half before breaking the solution seal and letting the fluid roll down without air bubbles. 'Can someone go out and wave down the ambulance so they know which house?'

'I'll go,' said Greg.

'Dennis, cut off Mitch's jeans, please.' She tightened a tourniquet around Mitch's upper arm and then flicked her fingers against his inner elbow. A vein rose up against her finger. 'Just the prick of a needle,' she said as she slid the cannula into place.

Mitch didn't even flinch. As she connected up the IV, the baby kicked her hard under the ribs. She rechecked the teenager's pulse, which was rapid, and took his blood pressure, which was low, and she ran the drip full bore. Where was the ambulance?

'Mitch, sorry, but I need to examine your groin.'

Fortunately, the teenager was now drugged up enough not to be embarrassed and she checked for bruising and bleeding around the scrotum and inguinal area that were often associated with a fractured pelvis.

Voices sounded down the hall and she swivelled around, welcoming the ambulance officers. 'Hi, guys. This is Mitch, aged seventeen, and he's fallen ten feet. Suspected fractured pelvis, left femur, right wrist and treating as a spinal injury until proven otherwise. I've given him morphine, put up a saline drip and he's stable, but I'm worried about a slow internal bleed.'

'Thanks, Doc, we can take it from here.' The older ambulance officer put the spinal board on the floor next to Mitch and started to connect the teenager up to the portable monitor.

'Mitch, I'll call your mum and swing by the hospital later to see you. Meanwhile, you're in good hands with these guys.'

'Okay.' He didn't sound very certain but no patient in shock ever did.

'Fellas, we need to give the ambos some space to do their job.'

Dennis put his hand out towards Georgie. She wasn't huge with the baby but as she'd been kneeling down for quite a while and her centre of balance was slightly off, she gratefully accepted his boost up.

They all walked into the dining room and while Dennis was giving her Mitch's mother's phone number, the plumber arrived.

'Hey, Dennis, we've got a bit of a problem.' Trevor rubbed his stubble-covered chin.

'You think?' replied the stressed-out builder. 'My apprentice is going to hospital and we've got a bloody big hole in the kitchen ceiling.'

'Yeah, I'll buy that.' Trevor puffed out an ironic laugh. 'But this is a different problem and you're not going to like it.'

Dennis opened another piece of nicotine gum and put it in his mouth with a sigh. 'What is it?'

'There's asbestos around the pipes and I've had a good look around. It's definitely in the walls as insulation and it might have been used in the roof.'

Dennis swore so violently that Georgie jumped.

'Asbestos in the roof? Where Mitch was? In all that dust that just fell down on him and us?' Georgie heard her rising incredulity but she didn't wait for a reply. Running back to the kitchen she said, 'Guys, possible asbestos contamination. Put on masks.'

The ambulance officers turned and stared at her and she found herself saying, 'Sorry. No one knew.'

'Lucky we travel with plenty of masks. Here.' The younger officer dug into his kit. 'Take one for everyone.'

'Thanks.' She took the masks and trudged back to the dining room, where she handed them out. 'Please wear these.'

When she gave one to Dennis, his face told her what she already knew—she'd have to move out.

His voice was muffled behind the mask. 'Doc, I'll have to arrange for a licensed asbestos-removal company to deal with this before we can come back in and work.'

No need to panic yet. 'And about how long will that take?'

'To ring the company? Two minutes. Until they can actually come and do the job?' He pulled on the scraggy ends of his beard. 'This close to Christmas and with the entire building industry shutting down for its annual holiday at the end of next week…' his shoulders rose and fell in defeat '…how long is a piece of string?'

She sucked in her lips and then breathed out slowly. 'So you're saying I might have to move out for more than a couple of days.'

'It will probably be more like a month. I can't really see this job happening until after New Year.'

Her mind grappled with dates. 'So you mean totally finished by early January rather than in two weeks? I can move back in the moment the asbestos is gone, right?'

He sighed, his expression resigned. 'I mean the asbestos will be removed early January and *then* we can come in and finish the job. Mid to late January.'

Her knees wobbled and she sat down on a chair as reality slugged her hard. She heard herself wail, 'But the baby's due on January twelfth.'

'Sorry, Doc. I know you want everything perfect for when the baby comes, but babies don't care about stuff like that. Hell, our firstborn slept in an old bottom drawer from a tallboy.' He grinned at the memory. 'We'd just moved again before the second and his room didn't get painted until he was two.'

'Dennis, if you're trying to reassure me, it isn't working.' Logistics raced around her mind and her heart rate matched their speed. She'd planned to finish up at work at the end of the week and spend the ten days before Christmas removing building dust and setting up the nursery. Now she was effectively homeless for weeks. None of this had been part of the plan. None of it was supposed to be happening. She was always so well organised and now all her best-laid plans were dust. Asbestos dust.

She bit off the rising stream of expletives that begged to pour from her lips, not just because her builder didn't need to know she could match him in that department but as part of practising for motherhood. Instead, she dropped her head in her hands and pressed her thumbs into her temples.

'I'm sure your family would love to have you stay with them at Christmas and fuss over you,' Dennis offered, hope in his voice.

'They're dead.' The words shot out, unexpectedly harsh, driven by her lack of control over the mess that was her house and the fact that the festive season was always a tough time for her without her parents.

Dennis's eyes widened. 'I didn't know. Sorry, love.'

'No, I'm sorry, Dennis.' She sat up straight, pulling herself together. 'You're trying to help and I appreciate it, but all in all today pretty much sucks.'

'Yeah, love, it does. How about you make this enforced time out of the house work for you?'

'What do you mean?'

'Take a bit of a holiday. Head down the coast because once the baby comes, you're going to be busy.'

The coast. An idea pinged into her head so big, bright and shiny that it was the answer to her problem. She shot to her feet and hugged the brawny builder. 'Dennis, you're brilliant.'

He grinned. 'Be sure to tell my wife that.'

She laughed. 'I will. You go and make that phone call and I'll go and pack a couple of suitcases.'

CHAPTER FOUR

HAMISH tipped the taxi driver and hefted his bag over his shoulder as he turned to gaze at the shimmering haze of purple blooms that illuminated the ancient jacaranda tree in his front garden. To him, the colour meant summer, Christmas and home. He still had the stench of Mumbai in his nostrils and he longed to replace it with the sharp tang of fresh salt air, but that would have to wait a bit longer, so for now he contented himself with a lungful of lemon-scented breeze, drifting over from the stand of white-barked eucalypts that grew across the road in the park.

Magpies, in their suits of black and white, stood on the nature strip, fixing their beady eyes on him and chortling as if acknowledging his absence and welcoming his return. He greeted them with a *'Coodle-loodle-do'*, fished his keys out of his backpack and bounded up the front steps. Sliding his key in the lock, he turned it, opened the door and called out, 'Honey, I'm home.' He promptly laughed at his own joke.

Twenty-four hours ago, just as he'd been preparing to leave India, he'd received a text from Georgie saying she hoped it was okay but she'd taken up his offer of a few days of R and R. He'd started texting his reply of *'No worries'*, but had stopped, deciding instead to surprise her. Although they'd been in contact with each other as much as usual, it had been a year since he'd last *seen* her—the afternoon she'd requested he be a sperm donor.

The fact they hadn't seen each other was his fault. After his three trips to the IVF clinic in Tasmania, the need to move had been so great that he'd put his hand up to co-ordinate an extra mission for Giving Back. He'd flown out to Ethiopia for three months. During that time he'd been on tenterhooks waiting for her to tell him she was pregnant.

When it didn't happen, the relief he'd experienced had been so strong and vibrant that he'd gone out and partied as if he'd just been reprieved from the gallows. He was off the hook. If she did get pregnant in the future, at least it wouldn't be from his sperm.

His return from Abbis Ababa had coincided with Georgie leaving for a beach holiday on Hamilton Island and by the time she'd returned, he'd left for India. Throughout the year she'd continued to post on his internet social network page and send her usual entertaining emails filled with funny and unusual stories about her work. She was equally interested in hearing about the challenges he faced co-ordinating the overseas trips of doctors who volunteered for Giving Back.

One thing he was certain of was that had she achieved a pregnancy from his donation, there'd be no way she'd be taking a mini-break in his house. She'd been as adamant as he that the baby was hers and hers alone.

'Hello? Who's there? Haim?'

He heard the hesitancy in her voice—her concern he might be an intruder—immediately followed by the accompanying creak of the third stair, and then he caught a glimpse of a shapely, tanned ankle followed by a toned calf. He smiled—she'd always had good legs. 'Yep, it's me.'

The clack of her sandals against the stairs sped up and a moment later there she was with her arms wide open and a matching smile. 'Welcome home.'

The bag he'd anchored on his shoulder with his hand

slipped past suddenly numb fingers, falling with a dull thud onto the floorboards as shock sucked the breath from his lungs. He instinctively shook his head as if the action would force his retinas to change the image. This couldn't be Georgie.

Apart from her voice, *nothing* about her was remotely familiar and he barely recognised her. Gone was her short-cropped hair and in its place a long, glossy, caramel-brown ponytail swept across her shoulders in a caress of curls. Her face, which had always seemed slightly too long for her, was now round and full. In fact, all of her was round and full. A white sundress fell from decorative shoulder straps, flowing across voluptuous breasts before cascading over a high and round belly and swirling against the enticing tilt of her hips, a curvaceous behind and firm thighs. She seemed taller, more sure of herself, and a secret smile played about her lips as if she knew things that others could never understand. She was a Botticelli woman—lush, fertile and glowing.

A thundering wave of pure sexual energy rode off her, spinning him into its orbit and rolling him inside its core. His groin tightened as a wondrous hot bolt of anticipation and excitement pounded through him—the same one he experienced whenever he saw a hot woman that he wanted. A familiar craving followed. A craving he greeted like an old but absent friend because for months it had rarely stirred, giving him an unfamiliar dry spell.

A second later his brain caught up with his body, its reaction horrified and stunned.

This is Georgie. Georgie. We're platonic. We made that decision years ago.

His body gave him the finger. It didn't care who she was, only that she was all woman and it wanted some of it. 'You...' His voice cracked over the husky word and he cleared his throat. 'You look good.'

'Thanks. I feel great and it was a good excuse for me to

get a whole new wardrobe.' Her velvet-brown eyes sparkled and her hand lightly caressed her belly, her palm cupping its rolling shape.

His gaze followed her movement and again his blood quickened, surging as another wave of need pulsed through him, numbing his brain. He couldn't construct a thought. Hell, he could barely see. He bit the inside of his cheek, needing the physical pain to short-circuit his arousal and get himself under control. His feet felt like lead weights glued to the floor and it was Georgie who leaned in, giving him a friendly kiss on the cheek and a quick hug. Her belly brushed gently against his stomach, the touch like an electric shock, jolting him out of the fog that had overtaken him.

She's pregnant. That's a baby in her belly. Baby!

Like a time-delay detonator on a bomb, the explosion of reality ripped through him, dousing arousal like an icy shower and bringing everything sharply into focus. His belief she'd never stay at the house if she was pregnant was instantly pulped.

Is it mine?

The question came out of nowhere, stunning him. He'd always said he never wanted to know; he'd totally believed he didn't want to know, but despite all that, his frantic gaze took in the tight package that was her belly and started calculating. She didn't look big but he was no obstetrician, and then he realised her size told him nothing because all women carried their babies differently and Georgie had always been fit and toned.

Dragging his hand through his overly long hair, he firmly told himself he *still* didn't want to know the answer, and yet he found he needed to work really hard not to voice the question. His gut churned against a leaden ball of contrary emotions that scared the hell out of him. Hating it all, he latched onto a rising resentment that she'd come to stay at his house when she'd promised him she wouldn't involve him in any way. 'You didn't tell me you were pregnant.'

Her rosy mouth tweaked up on one side at his accusatory tone. 'You said you didn't want blow-by-blow updates or ultrasound pictures.'

She had him there and irritation added to his shock, taking umbrage that she was not only at his house but not looking or seeming like his friend Georgie who'd he'd known and depended on for seventeen years. 'I didn't want minute details but I thought you'd at least tell me if it happened.'

'Really?' Her chestnut brows rose. 'I didn't get that impression from you at all. We both agreed that no matter what happened, this is my baby and there's no father, just an anonymous donor of sperm.'

His hands fisted by his sides as the unwanted question about paternity gained strength, despite his total agreement with her that it didn't matter who donated the sperm because the bottom line was it was *her* baby and it had nothing to do with him. 'So you're not going to tell me if I'm the donor?'

Her eyes filled with surprise and her top teeth snagged her bottom lip.

His gaze locked onto her lips as if this was the first time he'd seen them. He'd never realised how plump her bottom lip was or how together both lips peaked into a red bow that screamed to be unwrapped. *What the—?*

It was like he'd been plunged into a new world where everything hinted at being familiar but in reality it was all vastly different and totally foreign. Nothing was remotely recognisable—not Georgie's shape, not her sudden fashion sense and definitely not his insane reaction to her. Floundering like a man overboard waiting for a life-preserver, he ripped his gaze away from her mouth and focussed on her shoulder. 'Georgie, answer the question.'

'Are you sure you want to know?'

Yes. No. Damn it all. He ran his hand through his hair as

the question screamed in his head, refusing to be silenced. 'Just tell me so we can get it over with.'

She met his gaze, hesitation clear in her soft brown eyes. 'Thank you.'

Her quietly spoken words came with a sonic boom that deafened him. *It's mine.* His mouth dried and his stomach dropped. Signing papers and making a donation had been a clinical and detached process, but now, standing next to a glowing Georgie with a round belly, suddenly everything was starkly real and terrifying.

It's not my kid. I'm only a donor.

Anger—swift and strong—surged through him like a massive wave, swamping every other emotion in its path. 'I told you I didn't want anything to do with the baby and you agreed, so why on earth are you in my house?'

For a moment her shoulders drooped and he caught a glimpse of the Georgie he'd always known—uncertain about life, second-guessing everything and asking him for advice. Then her shoulders rolled back and she walked past him, all her uncertainty vanishing—absorbed by the new and more confident woman he barely recognised wearing a chic and *totally now* dress that made pregnancy look fashionable.

She flicked on the kettle. 'The short version is that the renovations revealed my house to be full of asbestos and I had to move out fast. You were overseas, your house was empty and you always say, "*Come and stay,*" so I did.' She seemed to draw in an extra-long breath and when she spoke her voice was higher than usual. 'If you'd let me know you were coming home, of course I would have left before you got here.'

Her reproachful tone poured fuel on his anger. 'It never occurred to me that you'd actually come here *pregnant.*'

She held his gaze but a flinch spiralled across her shoulders. 'I understand perfectly that you don't want any involvement and I do respect that. If you remember correctly, I don't want you involved either.' Her hands rolled over in supplication. 'I'm not here to argue with you, Hamish. Like I said, I didn't expect you home today. Now that you are, of course I'll move out.'

'Good.' It came out sharp and harsh and he saw the moment it lanced her with its painful impact and how her eyes filled with a wariness that had never been between them. A tiny part of him called out that he was being unfair but the rest of him was too angry with her to care.

Her chin shot up. 'I take it you'd prefer me to leave immediately rather than us having a normal, friendly, catch-up visit and a cup of tea first?'

The accusation in her voice that he was breaking the bonds of their friendship tore at him. He sat down, cross with himself, cross with her and generally out of sorts in his home, which was usually a peaceful and welcome haven.

He scrubbed at his face, his palms scratched by two days of travel stubble. 'I need something stronger than tea, George.'

'Knock yourself out,' she said ruefully, waving a packet of biscuits at him. 'I'll stick to my new vice.'

He pushed his chair back and walked over to the fridge, pulling a bottle of Mexican beer from the door and opening it with an overly hard twist. Taking a swig, he welcomed the river of cold streaming into his hot body and then took the bottle back to the table with him. Through the entire process his gaze kept sneaking glances at her pregnant belly and, like the rhythmic beat of an African drum, the words, *It's mine, it's mine*, kept playing over and over.

Shut up. I'm just a donor.

The sooner Georgie left and went back to Melbourne, the better. Out of sight was out of mind and once she was out of the house he'd stop thinking about the baby and her. Given his insane reaction to her pregnant body, he knew he needed to end his current sexual drought by going to a party as soon as possible so he could meet a pretty girl and have sex with her.

Like that worked so well for you last time you tried it nine months ago.

His body taunted him with a miserable memory and he shut it down fast. He heard Georgie sigh and a sudden thought had him saying, 'You *do* have somewhere else you can stay, right?'

Not really, no. Georgie sat down opposite Hamish, forcing her mouth into a reassuring smile as she soaked up the sight of him.

Lines of exhaustion splayed out around the edges of his eyes and charcoal rings of black smudged under the usually vivid but now weary blue. His hair, overdue for a haircut, had blond curls brushing the neckband of his T-shirt, giving him a boyish look that belied his thirty-six years.

Despite his fatigue and dishevelled appearance, he was still one of the most handsome men she'd ever laid eyes on. She'd always secretly basked in the fact that although a parade of much prettier women filled his life, she was his friend and she knew he always had a special smile reserved just for her.

Her heart dripped a tear of blood. Today she'd seen the moment his usual friendly delight had changed to horror, and how at times, when he looked at her belly, his expression twisted into something akin to disgust. It had torn through her, ripping and burning, and as much as she'd loved staying here, she knew she had to leave because to stay might cause a permanent crack in their friendship. She wasn't convinced that crack hadn't already formed because she'd never known him to be so ticked off with her.

If she could have wound back the clock, she would have. She'd always known that staying here had verged on pushing their friendship, but desperate times and a lioness's desire to protect her baby had made her take the risk. Now it had all backfired horribly.

'George?'

She fiddled with the loose edge on a Balinese woven placemat. 'I'll make some calls. It will work out just fine.'

His mouth flattened. 'It's a tricky time of year, with the school holidays starting and Christmas not far away.' He pulled a business card from his wallet and snapped it down in front of her, the action both reluctant and purposeful. The bold pink-and-white logo declared the name of a real-estate agency. 'Call Chris and mention my name. He might be able to help you.'

'Okay, thanks.'

He sipped his beer silently as his animosity cloaked her. She fought to think of a neutral topic so they could find their usual camaraderie. 'You look wiped out and exhausted.'

'Yeah.' He traced his fingers through the condensation that had dribbled off the beer bottle, making a ring of water on the table.

She pushed on. 'Tough trip?'

'No. Great trip.' Suddenly his demeanour changed and the spark of enthusiasm for life that usually glowed so brightly in his eyes returned. 'Giving Back's "Operation Grin" assessed two hundred children, corrected seventy-five cleft palates and did thirty facial reconstructions for burns victims. We brought two children back with us who need ongoing surgery.'

'That's sensational.' She leaped onto the topic, pushing away the question that popped up in her mind often. The one that asked, *How can he work with children and not want one of his own?* 'How did all those plastic surgeons feel about being organised by a mere accident and emergency doctor?'

He grinned. 'I let them think they were in charge.'

She laughed. Her Hamish was back.

He's not yours, remember? He never has been.

Once Hamish started talking about Giving Back, he tended not to draw breath for quite some time. He gesticulated widely as he told her of the highs and lows of the trip, and she let his words wash over her, pretending that things were fine between them and that the existence of the baby wouldn't change a thing.

'I need a shower and a catnap.' He stood up abruptly and inclined his head towards the phone.

She took the hint. 'I'll pack and make some calls.'

'Good idea.' He seemed to hesitate for a moment and then he leaned in towards her.

She turned in surprise and suddenly his warm, firm lips pressed half against her cheek and half against the edge of her mouth. His heady scent of sweat and fading cologne swirled around her and she found herself breathing in harder, as if absorbing a part of him. She welcomed the faint prickle of his whiskers lightly tickling her lips and the friendly tingle of warmth that slowly roved through her slumbering body in a reassuring way.

Our friendship's safe. Everything's is going to be okay.

His mouth moved again and for the briefest of moments their lips covered each other's and his taste of hops and malt flooded her mouth. Flooded her body.

Comforting warmth exploded into fire and her body jerked awake as primal need rushed through her, making her body beg for more. Every pulse point throbbed, the apex of her thighs ached and it was a miracle that she managed to stop the guttural moan of need that rose in her throat.

Then he was walking away from her, saying, 'Let yourself out, won't you?' And he disappeared from view.

Her legs collapsed from under her and she sat down hard, hating her body as much as she ever had. She knew pregnancy hormones got blamed for all sorts of things but she didn't know they could be responsible for wildly inaccurate lust. Not even back in the early days of being friends when she'd thought about Hamish in a sexual way had her body experienced such intensity.

We are friends. Just friends.

She blew out some long, deep breaths and got herself under control. Pregnant women didn't think about sex, or at least that's what she'd been told by some pregnant women in relationships, and she'd agreed with them because right up to this point her libido had been dormant for the entire pregnancy, although she had noticed she rolled her shoulders back a touch more and was actually proud of her body for the first time ever.

Still, this reaction to Hamish was so unexpected it had to be an aberration. A crazy blip brought on by stress and the fact she was homeless again.

The only thing she should be thinking about right now was finding a place to live, and with that thought firmly in place she picked up the phone and dialled the real-estate agent.

Hamish woke up from his nap as the late-afternoon sun sneaked in under the awning and spilled over his bed in a hot spot. With a groan, he rolled over and glanced at the clock. Five o'clock. Three hours since he'd kissed Georgie. Three hours since he'd spent five minutes in a cold shower getting rid of the effects of that ill-thought-out kiss. One minute he had been prevaricating about whether to give her his usual farewell peck on the cheek because he was still so mad at her, and the next minute he'd wanted to stick his tongue in her mouth and greedily take his fill of her taste of peppermint and heat, which hovered seductively on her lips, promising so much more.

He pulled the pillow over his head in disgust at the memory. Disgust at himself. Thank God Georgie had left the house. He didn't understand what the hell was going on with him and he didn't trust himself not to do something stupid and irretrievable. Whether it was jet-lag or not, the only solution he could see was to avoid seeing her until after her baby was born. Only then would she be back to being the

Georgie he'd always relied on rather than the fecund tempt-
ress she was now.

Even then, he'd make sure Georgie arranged for a babysitter when they caught up. He wasn't *ever* having anything
to do with the baby. Didn't she know kids caused parents irreparable heartache? He'd seen and lived through the damage.

He swung his feet to the floor and tugged on some shorts
before pulling on a faded T-shirt. His stomach gurgled, reminding him he needed to shop first and then eat something.
As he opened his bedroom door, the rumble of his father's
voice and the tinkling lilt of his mother's drifted up the stairs.
Grinning, he ran down, calling out a loud, 'Hello,' and met
his parents as they walked out of his lounge room.

'Good to see you, Hamish.' His father pumped his hand,
before pulling him into a quick bear hug cum thump on the
back.

His mother kissed him and then hugged him tightly as she
gave a short sniff. 'I'm glad you're home safe.'

He kissed her back. 'You don't have to worry so much,
Mum.'

His father's big laugh held the remnants of old pain. 'All
part of the parent territory, son.'

And yet despite their firsthand experience, they wondered
why he hadn't chosen to settle down and have a family of his
own. It was a conundrum he could never quite fathom, given
what had happened all those years ago with Aaron. Given
his role in his brother's death.

'It's great to see you both. What brings you to town?'

His mother clucked her tongue. 'We're shopping for
Christmas and the reunion.'

He must have looked blank because she rolled her eyes at
him, and suddenly he was whisked back in time to when he'd
been fourteen, battling hormones and totally disorganised.

'Right. The reunion.' Saying the words wasn't quite
enough to kick-start his memory, and as his parents were in

their mid-sixties, reunions seemed to punctuate their lives. 'Which reunion is it? Nursing? Dad's Antarctic crew?'

'Hamish, how can you have forgotten? I've sent you emails and one of those reminder things that goes straight into your phone,' she said, her voice combining frustration with resignation. 'Honestly, sometimes I swear the men in my life are deaf. It's the huge ten-year family reunion we're hosting at the guesthouse and it starts Saturday. You *promised* me you'd be there.'

A memory stirred through his weariness.

'Denise, my darling, cut the boy some slack. He's half-asleep and jet-lagged.' His dad gave her shoulder an affectionate squeeze and he threw Hamish a *best to just agree* look. 'Isn't that right, son?'

'Sorry, Mum.' He winked at his father. 'I promise to remember everything as soon as I've eaten.'

'You haven't eaten?' Denise's demeanour changed instantly.

His mother's idea of happiness was cooking and feeding people, which was why she'd started the guesthouse. In Denise Pettigrew's mind there were few problems in life that couldn't be solved by good food and a conversation.

Hamish was never totally sure whether it was therapy for herself or for others, but of one thing he was certain—his mother could never resist the words *I'm hungry*. Occasionally he'd uttered them just to distract her so a subject could be changed or dropped.

'You poor thing,' she clucked. 'Travelling all that way and no lunch?' She bustled him towards the kitchen, saying, 'Why didn't you have lunch with Georgina?'

He stopped so abruptly that his mother walked into him. 'You met Georgie?' His normally deep voice came out as a squeak and silver spots danced before his eyes.

'Yes. She was here when we arrived.' His mother moved past him, smiling.

Was here. Was. Past tense, ergo she is now gone. The screaming noise of abject anxiety subsided and his fast-beating heart slowed. With forced casualness he shoved his hands into his pockets and recommenced walking.

'It was lovely to see her again,' Denise said. 'I don't understand why you didn't tell us she was pregnant.'

'I didn't know,' he muttered. At least he didn't have to lie.

'Such a shame about her house,' his father said.

Disquiet skittered through him, ramping up the smouldering ashes of his unease. Roy Pettigrew was an ex-high-school principal and despite a new career in tourism he still had a tendency to collect waifs and strays.

'We've been helping her with the phone calls.'

Nausea pitched his stomach like a boat on a stormy sea. Surely Georgie wasn't still here? She couldn't be. She'd promised to leave. He stumbled forward and a second later a surge of acid—driven up on wave of dread—burned the back of his throat, filling his mouth with a metallic taste.

Georgie sat at the table with her phone pressed to her ear with one hand and tapping a pen against a notepad with her other hand. Deep furrows of concentration creased her high forehead and very slowly she moved her gaze towards him. Her eyes met his—round and soft like a puppy's and filled with a mixture of regret, guilt and steely purpose.

Every expletive he'd ever heard in his life hit his lips at high velocity and it took every ounce of his unravelling self-control to swallow them back down unuttered. God help him, Georgie and his parents were in the *same* room.

Damn it, Georgie, you shouldn't be here.

Her regret and guilt didn't touch the pure, hot anger that burned inside him and for the second time that day—for the second time in his life—he was furious with his best friend. She'd put him in an unconscionable position and her being here with his parents was his worst nightmare.

He had to separate them. He had to get them as far away

from each other as possible and it had to be done fast, and without his parents realising what he was doing.

How? His mind seemed stalled and devoid of ideas. Rushing his parents out the door would only generate more questions—questions he didn't want to answer. To avoid that, his parents had to stay, which only left him with one option. Georgie had to leave. Hell, she should have left three hours ago and she knew it.

As Georgie ended her call, his father immediately asked, 'Any luck, dear?'

'Not yet.' She crossed a name off a long list written in blue pen. Red strike lines dominated the page.

'I'm not surprised.' Denise donned an apron and started dicing an onion. 'This close to Christmas all accommodation's at a premium. Most people book months in advance.'

'Have you spoken to Chris?' Hamish finally found his voice but it came out curt despite the steadying breath he'd taken first. He caught his parents exchanging a look.

Georgie's Christmas-bow mouth flattened and her eyes flashed. 'Of course I've spoken to him. And Rachel, Tiffany, Erica, James and...' she consulted her list '...Jeff and Doug. But your mum's right. There's nothing available and I'm at the point of ringing motels.'

'That's a—'

'You can't stay at a motel,' Denise cut him off in a horrified voice.

If a motel got Georgie away from his parents then so be it. 'Georgie's a grown-up, Mum. She can do whatever she wants.'

Denise slammed the frying-pan down hard on his ceramic stovetop and Roy raised his bushy eyebrows at Hamish, disappointment shining clear in his pale blue eyes.

'It will be fine, Mrs Pettigrew,' Georgie said, sounding far from fine. 'It's just for a few weeks.'

'A few weeks is a long time in your condition, dear. I'm sure there's another solution.'

Hamish dodged his mother's glance. She had no idea what was going on and it had to stay that way. 'Georgie should be in Melbourne so she can supervise her renovations.'

'Melbourne's expensive and frantic at this time of year with Christmas and all the summer sporting events,' Roy said.

Hamish gritted his teeth. 'So is the coast, Dad.'

'I've got a building supervisor and nothing's happening with the house until after Christmas,' Georgie said. 'At this point I'll travel *anywhere* I can find a place but there's nothing. The three of us have been at this all afternoon and we keep drawing blanks.' Her hand fluttered over her baby bump and she flashed him a look filled with guilt, regret and desperation that said, *You have to believe me.*

'Well, there's more than one way to skin a cat,' said Roy. 'We just need to put our heads together.'

'I know,' said Denise, her face creasing into a smile. 'I don't know why we didn't think of this before. You should stay here.'

No, no, no, no, no. 'Mum, that isn't going to work.'

Denise frowned slightly. 'Why not?'

For reasons I can't tell you. But he knew his mother and without a watertight reason she would push this until she got her own way. *Think.* Desperation finally forced his brain into action and he hauled out his phone, bringing up his reminders and scrolling through them frantically.

Bingo.

'Because I've arranged for the floors to be sanded while I'm at the reunion. No one, let alone a pregnant woman, should be breathing in polyurethane fumes. The house will be out of action for at least a week.'

'Is everyone renovating this summer?' Georgie's voice sounded strangled, as if she was fighting not to cry.

For the first time he noticed the lines of worry around her eyes, and guilt burrowed into his anger with her. It wasn't her fault her house was a disaster zone, and he sighed. 'Sorry, George. I'm happy to pay for your motel accommodation.' *Anything for you to be as far away as possible from my parents.*

In a heartbeat Georgie's spine went from slumped to ramrod stiff. 'That won't be necessary. I'm perfectly capable of paying my own way, thank you.'

Her clipped words whipped him and he hated it that they made him feel petty, but there was no way he could afford to have her spend any time with his parents.

'It's settled, then.' Roy nodded at Denise, who returned it with a smile of mutual understanding.

It always amazed him that his parents seemed to have a secret code of communication that he could never fathom. 'Nothing's settled, Dad.'

Roy ignored him. 'Georgie, we have a large guesthouse and although it's about to be filled with generations of Pettigrews from around the country, if you can cope with a crowd, there's a bed at Weeroona for as long as you need it.'

No way in hell. Blind panic roared through his veins, closing his throat and freezing his mind. He stared at Georgie, willing her to remember one of the three things he'd asked of her a year ago when he'd signed those bloody donor papers.

Georgie stared at Roy as if she couldn't believe her ears. 'Oh, Roy, that's very kind of you, but I couldn't possibly impose on you and your family.'

Thank you, Georgie. His breathing slowed.

Denise shook her head emphatically. 'It's not an imposition at all. The more the merrier.'

'That's right. If you're worried about not being family we'll just say you're a second cousin twice removed.' Roy joked. 'We have lots of those. But, seriously, as Denise and I are the hosts, it really doesn't matter what anyone else thinks. You are our guest.'

Cut this off at the knees. 'Mum, Dad, she's pregnant and Jindi's too far from Melbourne.' Hamish used the authoritative tone that made new Emergency interns quake.

'Doctors.' Roy shook his head as if Hamish knew nothing. 'Son, babies are born in worse places than the Jindi River Bush Hospital. You and your brothers were born there and you turned out just fine.' He turned back to Georgie. 'It's a lovely little hospital and I'm on the board. If there's any chance that the baby might arrive while you're with us, it will be well cared for.'

'There's no NICU, Georgie,' Hamish growled, hoping the warning in his voice was so clear that she'd give his parents' invitation an emphatic and final *no*.

'Hamish?' His mother stared at him with a confused look on her face. 'You've told us stories about delivering babies in Africa where you were lucky to have a pair of gloves, and Jindi Hospital is well equipped for normal births.' She faced Georgina. 'I don't want to pry, dear, but I'm sensing the father of this baby isn't on the scene?'

Hamish's lungs cramped.

Georgie glanced down at her lap, bit her lip and silently shook her head.

He breathed again.

Denise continued talking. 'And there isn't anyone else you can go to?'

The noose, which had been looped loosely around Hamish's neck from the moment he'd found Georgie still here, tightened so fast he coughed. In his parents' eyes Georgie had just gone from a woman needing some assistance to a stray needing their protection and care. In utter desperation he yelled, 'Did it ever occur to you, Mum, that Georgie might just want to be on her own?'

The words hung in the air like toxic slime—only he was the one who was contaminated.

His parents looked at him as if they didn't recognise him or his behaviour, and then Denise turned back to Georgie. 'You're alone, homeless and pregnant at Christmas, dear. You need to come home with us.'

Georgie shot to her feet as fast as a pregnant woman could. 'I really don't want to inconvenience any of you, least of all be the cause of a family argument. Something will turn up and, honestly, Mrs Pettigrew, you don't have to worry about me. I'm a big girl and very capable of looking after myself.'

His parents stayed silent but their eyes spoke volumes. Even without their disapproving looks Hamish's own guilt at how he'd been prepared to abandon her to a motel was eating at him. They were both victims of the overactive Pettigrew social conscience and neither of them had stood a chance. Unhappily, he picked up Georgie's bags. 'It looks like you're coming to Jindi.'

Georgie didn't say anything but her huge brown eyes filled with entreaty. Her shoulders rose and fell as if to say, *I am so sorry*, and the pendant she wore dipped into the generous cleavage created by her now-fuller breasts.

An image of his face buried where the pendant rested shot into his mind and sweat beaded on his forehead. He grappled for control and at that very moment he hated her. Where had his friend gone?

He hated it that her body had changed so much that he now noticed every little thing about her. He hated it that every time he looked at her he got hot and hard and wanted to explore every inch of that lush, round and feminine body. But most of all he hated it that she'd broken his trust and put the three of them of them smack bang in the heart of his family.

He could never forgive her for that.

CHAPTER FIVE

THE raucous squawk of a flock of crimson rosellas made Georgie look up into the dawn sky, and she caught the flash of red and blue plumage as they launched themselves from the massive gumtree. Unable to sleep, she'd risen as the first rays of sun had peeked over the horizon and had set off on an early-morning walk. Although she was surrounded by nature, which was supposed to be soothing, she felt anything but calm. She rubbed her stomach. 'Oh, Widget, what a mess.'

Last night, apart from issuing the occasional instruction, Hamish hadn't spoken a single word to her on the two-hour drive to Jindi River, and just to make sure she didn't talk he'd turned up the music to prevent any conversation. From the moment his parents had left the house, she'd tried to apologise to him, but he hadn't acknowledged it in any shape or form and his rigid body had radiated waves of antagonism that had told her in no uncertain terms that she was *persona non grata*.

Part of her didn't blame him for his anger. She should have stood her ground against his parents' increasing insistence that she come to Jindi and instead insisted on her bags being loaded into her car. Equally, she should have driven back to Melbourne and begged for a bed at one of her colleagues' homes, despite the fact she doubted any of their wives would have been thrilled because of the busy time of year.

So many *should-haves*. The bottom line was that the cumulative effects of three hours of constant searching for a place to stay had made her bone-weary, anxious and miserable.

All of it had collided with an overwhelming need to protect her unborn child, which had been compounded by feeling totally alone and missing her parents desperately. In short, she'd allowed Roy and Denise's concern to wrap around her like a favourite and comforting blanket on a cold night, and as a result her resistance had been token at best. So, yes, she understood Hamish's anger at her but she was pretty disappointed with the juvenile way he'd dealt with it. If he thought he could just ignore her and freeze her out, he was sadly mistaken. They'd been friends for too long for that sort of nonsense.

No, the only way to sort this mess out was by talking, but even she knew that waking up a sleeping man to 'talk' was unwise, as was trying to talk to a man before his early-morning surf. It was for those reasons she was out on an exploratory walk to pass the time before breakfast. Denise had told her breakfast was usually served at eight, but this morning it would be a self-serve affair because the 'Pettigrew mob', as she referred to the reunion, would be arriving over the next two days.

It had been dark last night when Hamish had silently parked the car but the dawn had revealed Weeroona—in all her restored Edwardian grandeur—nestled in beautiful bushland. She was an elegant lady, evoking a bygone era and a style of holiday that was now long gone. Limestone walls streaked with gold and white sand gleamed against the red-brick framed windows. The broad sweeping roof with its six enormous brick chimneys spread down to incorporate a wide upstairs veranda and the gum-grey wood-turned veranda poles supported the cream gingerbread fretwork that graced the front of the building.

A well-maintained lawn surrounded the house but it stopped abruptly at the base of towering mountain ash and beech trees, as if civilisation could only stretch so far. A stile in the fence marked where the property stopped and the dense state forest began. Georgie was amazed that she was surrounded by trees and yet she was only a short ten-minute drive away from the Great Southern Ocean and the glorious coastline. Weeroona had the sea at the front door and rainforest at the back. No wonder Hamish loved it here.

Hamish. As she clambered back over the stile, she heard the splintering sound of an axe against wood. Someone was up. She followed the sound, walking past a shed and into the utilities area off to the left of the back door. Hamish stood in a well-worn clearing, shirtless and with his back to her. He heaved an axe high above his head before bringing it down hard and fast onto small logs, splitting them into kindling.

The sunlight glittered golden in his hair and the muscles of his tanned back bunched and released with the action, the movement rippling down his torso, through strong legs smattered with blond hair and finishing at his workboot-covered feet.

It was poetry in motion—a rhythmic feast—and she stared at him as if her retinas were glued to the centre of his wide, broad back. She'd always admired his athleticism and had often hung back, waiting for another wave, just so she could watch him surf. He had a natural ease in everything—a sort of perfect confidence that said, *Look out, world, I'm here.* It was one of the things she loved about him—probably because that sort of easy confidence was the polar opposite of herself, although since becoming pregnant she'd noticed she stood up for herself more because it meant standing up for the baby.

He tossed the kindling into a growing pile and as he bent down to pick up the next log, his shorts clung to his taut behind, creating the perfect outline. Her curling fingers suddenly pressed into her palms. She gasped as a river of heat swooped through her so fast it set off a chain reaction, starting with her nipples tingling hard and finishing with an aching and tantalising throb between her legs.

Oh, God, not again.

He turned round and the moment he saw her his face hardened. 'Oh, it's you.'

'Yes.' His total lack of enthusiasm at seeing her acted like a bucket of cold water on the slow burn of unprecedented lust.

'You're up early.'

Without thinking, she said, 'The baby's often active at dawn.'

He glared at her, his eyes blazing with undisguised animosity, and then he turned away and slammed the axe so hard into the log that wood splintered everywhere.

It jolted every particle of lust from her body and she was left with a hollow feeling in her gut, as if she'd just lost something really precious. 'Hamish, how long are you going to behave like a ten-year-old who got run out in back-yard cricket?'

The axe came down with another thwack. 'For as long as I want. I'm not the one at fault here.'

She tried a smile, hoping it would trickle into her voice. 'You never told me that your parents are a *force majeure*. Who stands a chance against that sort of teamwork, right?'

Thwack.

She bit her lip. 'Is it really such a bad thing that I'm here?'

He dropped the axe and stalked toward her with eyes flashing. 'Yes.'

If he'd slapped her cheek it would not have hurt as much. 'You've broken the promise you made me.'

A surge of self-righteous indignation had her shaking her head quickly. She was innocent of that particular charge. 'I haven't broken any promises to you. *Ever*. Not in seventeen years, including the time you rang me to fill in for you at work after you sneaked an extra day off to go skiing and then got snowed in at Mt. Hotham. To this day, hospital Admin thinks you got struck down with a forty-eight-hour stomach upset and your reputation as "Mr Reliable" is still intact.'

The shared memory she hoped would crack a smile from him didn't even dent the tension in his jaw. 'I asked that my parents never find out about—'

'And they won't,' she rushed to reassure him, feeling exactly the same way about the Pettigrews not finding out because it would destroy her friendship with Hamish and complicate her life and the baby's.

'How do you figure that?' His wide fingers dragged through his hair. 'You're pregnant with a kid that shares half my DNA, you're staying at my parents' home and soon to be surrounded by my very large extended family. How is that not breaking a promise?'

They'd disagreed about things before but she'd never experienced hostility from him, and it took all her resolve not to instinctively step backwards from the intense look of dislike in his eyes. Nothing about him was the Hamish she knew, and every part of her wanted to banish that look. She wanted her friend back.

'Haim, I promised you that your parents would never find out you were the father of the baby and I will uphold that promise and never tell them.'

A muscle in his jaw throbbed. 'Do you promise on a blood pact?'

She stared at him, thinking he must be joking. 'What are we? Twelve?'

He didn't smile.

She sighed. 'I'm beyond sorry that I'm here but you have to know I didn't plan any of it. My plan, and you know how I love to plan, got derailed by things totally out of my control. I'd give anything to be settled in my house, doing some heavy-duty nesting.'

'So would I.'

A zip of annoyance shot through her and she wanted to

shake him but she crossed her arms instead. She'd spent enough time with him to know that living to the beat of his own drum for years had given Hamish a tendency to want things to go his way.

'Haim, I've said sorry enough and I'm not saying it again so you need to build a bridge and get over it. I'm not prepared for my baby and me to be homeless so I'm staying as your parents' guest, and you have to find a way to deal with that.'

His high forehead registered shock at her tone, but she kept talking. 'There's *no* reason for Denise and Roy to connect you with the baby because we've never even dated, but the one sure-fire way to make them suspicious is for you to keep acting like a petulant child and freezing me out.'

'I'm not being petulant,' he said sulkily.

She raised her brows. 'Yeah, right. If you say so.'

He stared at her for a long moment, his cornflower-blue eyes swirling with a thousand varieties of shocked surprise, tinged with worry and with something else she was having trouble decoding.

'Have you quite finished, George?'

'Only if you've heard me.'

He threw up his hands in surrender. 'Okay, point taken. Yes, I've been acting on the wrong side of crazy but, hell, can you see *my* point? My parents can't find out. If they even get a hint that the baby is a Pettigrew, your dreams of having sole control will be shot to pieces.'

She rubbed her belly, forcing away the soothing feelings that Roy and Denise's concern had generated last night. She knew they didn't belong to her and the baby in any way because the Pettigrews weren't her parents and her loyalty lay with Hamish. 'Please stop worrying. Widget and I will never tell.'

For the first time in the conversation his face relaxed into its familiar and smiling lines. 'What did you just call it?'

She grinned at him, relief flooding her that he was back

to looking more like her Hamish with dimples swirling. 'Widget. It's a placeholder in manufacturing.'

He shoved his hands into his pockets and rubbed the dirt with the steel-capped toe of his boot. 'So you haven't found out the sex?'

His question surprised her because it showed an unexpected element of interest in the baby. 'No. I figure I have hours of hard work ahead of me so I want a surprise at the end.'

'Fair enough, although given the Pettigrew family history, it's likely to be a boy.'

'Really?'

'Really. In this line of Pettigrews no girl's been born in five generations.' He stepped in close and gave her shoulder a squeeze. 'Sorry I wigged out.'

She nodded, wanting to leave the subject behind and move onto more settled ground—the one where their friendship was cemented back into place. 'I'm famished. Do you think we could do an early raid on breakfast?'

'I've got a better idea. Let's drive into Jindi and hit the bakery. They bake the best Christmas stollen and mince pies, and after we've filled up on those we can check out the swell. If the waves are running there'll be just enough time for a quick surf before my brothers and their families arrive.'

She glanced at her belly and back at him. 'Not really sure surfing's an option for me this year, mate.'

He winked at her. 'You can watch me.'

Damn it, did he know she did that? Horrified that he might have also noticed that she'd been sneaking glances at him over the past twenty-four hours, she lifted her chin and called on mock superiority. 'In that case, I'll have a list of coaching tips for you when you come back to shore.'

'You wish.'

His big, bold laugh boomed around her, wrapping her in reassurance. She relaxed into it, totally unprepared for the tingling chaser that hit without warning. She tried not to let his twinkling blue eyes pull her gaze into the depths of his, while she unsuccessfully fought the flutter of wondrous sensation that was rapidly spreading through her. The moment it dived deep, setting up an addictive throb of need in its wake, she wanted to sway forward and press her lips against his, desperate to feel the burn of his heat on her mouth like she had yesterday.

Stop right now. Pregnancy hormone alert. Bad idea.

She glued her heels to the ground with common sense and steadied herself. She and Hamish were mates and she'd put their friendship on shaky ground with the baby and coming to Weeroona. She didn't need to stress it even more by adding inappropriate lust into the mix. That would make things beyond awkward.

'You okay?'

She nodded overly hard. 'Fine. Just hungry. Can we go to the bakery right now?'

'Sure.' He raised his arm as if he was about to sling it across her shoulders, as he often did, but then he dropped it back by his side.

The sear of disappointment burned right through her, leaving behind a smouldering emptiness. There was truth in the adage that actions spoke louder than words, and when she combined it with the new look in his eye every time he looked at her, she realised that although he'd said he'd forgiven her, she wasn't certain he'd spoken the truth.

'Uncle Hamish, come and play cricket.'

'Only if I bat first.' He teasingly pulled Jack's hat down over the nine-year-old boy's eyes, enjoying his annual visit with his nephews, although this year with the reunion it was longer than usual.

Jack adjusted his hat and shot Hamish a look that said, *Get real.* 'Da's batting first, then Dad, then Uncle Caleb, then...' Jack listed off the Pettigrew men in age order.

'What about Opa? He usually opens.'

Jack shrugged. 'He said he's umpiring this year.'

Hamish glanced over to the makeshift cricket pitch on the expansive back lawn and saw his grandfather sitting on a chair in clear sight of the bails. At eighty-five he was fit and spry and although for the past few years he'd used one of his great-grandsons—there being no great-granddaughters—to run for him, he'd usually belted out quite a few sixes before going out. The fact he'd chosen to sit out the Pettigrew cricket cup and not bat for the Jindi River mob gave Hamish pause.

It was the afternoon of the second day of the reunion and seventy-five descendents of Hattie and George Pettigrew, aged from thirteen months to ninety-five years, were installed in the multiplicity of rooms. Weeroona was full and his mother was in seventh heaven. He'd spent yesterday showing his various relatives to their rooms and helping with luggage and being a general 'gofer' for his parents. Since his early-morning visit yesterday to the beach, he hadn't seen much of Georgie. Out of sight, however, was not out of mind. God, he wished it was, but Georgie had moved into his head and he couldn't shift her.

He'd tried, man, how he'd tried. He'd spent time with his brothers, kept himself busy with a thousand mundane tasks set by his mother—including hauling the massive pine tree into the foyer and setting it by the stairs ready for the kids to decorate it. He'd even done jobs that in the past he would have happily delegated to his brothers and nephews, but despite filling his time to the hilt he hadn't managed to quiet the barrage of buzzing thoughts about Georgie that bounced and leapt in his head in a never-ending loop.

It was as if a pregnant impostor with a take-charge attitude and a body for sin had moved in and his Georgie—the slightly unsure-of-herself woman with an attractive but not overtly sexual body—had completely vanished. Everything about their friendship that he'd taken for granted had changed.

Apart from the night they'd graduated, when the combination of exhilaration and champagne had fuelled a misguided deep kiss and they'd both agreed that going any further would be totally the wrong thing to do, he'd taught himself to only ever think of Georgie as his best friend who he loved spending time with. Now, whenever they met, he saw a voluptuous and sexy woman who sent such a strong visceral craving through him that it made his head spin and his groin ache.

Big-figured women had *never* been his style and neither had lusting after Georgie, so his reaction made no sense and his confusion duelled with his increasing desire for her. The fact she was pregnant with a baby he wanted nothing to do with should have had his body sexually dormant from within a sixty-kilometre radius of her. Only his body had other plans and last night it had added 3D dreams to the mix and he'd woken up hot, hard and more frustrated than ever. As he'd stood under a cold shower, his newly hatched plan to deal with all of this was to think *baby* every time he saw Georgie.

As the idea of being a father was his worst nightmare that would surely shock his body back into its normal rhythm. That and meeting a slim, twenty-something blonde on the beach at Jindi.

'James can't umpire,' said his first cousin Richard, walking towards him. 'He's hardly impartial and he'll rule against the Omeo mob.'

Hamish grinned at Richard's faux indignation, happy to let the unsettling thoughts of Georgie slide as he got busy with the good-natured sledging that was as much a part of the Pettigrew cricket cup as the actual game.

'The umpire's the least of your mob's problems, Rich. I'd be more worried about the fact your ace bowler is glued to his phone and constantly texting his girlfriend rather than warming up.'

'Seth will be fine.' Richard winked. 'Think of all that fifteen-year-old sexual frustration he'll be channelling into the game. I'm tipping Jindi will be all out for thirty-five.'

Hamish thought about his own frustrations. 'In your dreams, mate.'

But Richard's attention had moved from Hamish and he blew out a low whistle as he cocked his head. 'Why is it I've never met *that* particular distant cousin?'

Hamish followed his gaze and sweat broke out on his top lip. Georgie was walking across the grass, barefoot, hips swaying and holding a green parasol over her head as shade against the summer sun. She'd scooped her hair up on top of her head, exposing her neck and shoulders, which were almost bare except for the slash of two red straps that connected with the rest of her dress at the swell of her breasts.

The soft fabric flowed around her compact baby bulge, although from where they stood it would have been hard to tell if she was pregnant or very full figured.

What was obvious was the sexual energy that poured off her in tantalising waves—that *I'm all woman and my body is doing what it was born to do, and doing it well* energy. The intoxicating energy that had him constantly hot, cold and hard was now making Richard take notice of her too.

Richard loved women, and an unanticipated protective flare went through Hamish, making him speak without thinking. 'That's Georgie, and she's off limits.'

At his warning growl, a competitive glint entered his cousin's eyes and the years rolled back in an instant to the bygone summers of their teenage years. The long, hot summers they'd spent on the beach besting each other in all sorts of ways from surfing and skiffle boarding to who could get the prettiest girls to kiss them first. And they'd kept score.

Richard grinned. 'I might just go over and introduce myself.'

Hamish frowned. He knew Richard and he'd just inad-

vertently thrown down a challenge the man wouldn't be able
to refuse.

*Does it matter? Georgie's been taking care of herself for
years.*

But for some crazy reason it did matter and he thought
fast to repair the damage. With studied casualness he said,
'Go right ahead. The more distracted the Omeo team is on
the field, the better.' He matched Richard's grin. 'I can picture the Pettigrew cup on Weeroona's mantelpiece now, can't
you, Jack?'

'That would be ace, Uncle Hamish.'

'Don't go counting the runs before they've happened,
Jacko,' said Richard, slapping the boy playfully on the back.
'Let's play cricket.'

Hamish let go of a breath he hadn't been aware he'd been
holding and walked to the pitch where his father declared that
Jindi had lost the toss and Omeo had elected to bat.

Ninety minutes later the Omeo mob was still in and
Richard was batting. Hamish stood on the boundary because
Richard was known to hit sixes, but so far he'd only returned
one ball as most were going into midfield. With not a lot to
do, his attention kept inexplicably straying to Georgie. She'd
settled in a chair next to Opa and was balancing a notepad
on her knees. Roy had asked her to co-umpire and provide
the impartiality that no Pettigrew could. Hamish wasn't sure
how much she knew about cricket but so far no one had ob-
jected to her calls.

A cheer went up from the Omeo mob and Hamish realised
he had no clue what had just happened.

Caleb caught his eye and tilted his head towards Richard
and the message was clear—Hamish had to get his head
into the game.

He took charge, shouting out some fielding changes to
his team—bringing his father in closer to the wickets and
placing the kids evenly around the boundary. They needed

to get Richard out as soon as possible or Omeo would get extra points at the end of the twentieth over.

Big brother Ben commenced bowling and considerably slowed Richard's run rate but after three overs he still hadn't bowled him out. Hamish moved the kids into silly mid-on.

Ben spoke to his son. 'Jack, you're up. Give it your best shot.'

Hamish had to admire the nine-year-old's style, and he was struck by how similar his gait and bowling action were to Ben's. As the baby brother of the family, Hamish had spent a lot of Saturdays being dragged to country cricket matches and he was familiar with all aspects of Ben's technique. Jack had it all plus a hint of dazzle, and he wondered if it was nature or nurture. Was the kid good because he too had been watching his father play since birth or was it a Pettigrew cricket gene given opportunity?

What will Georgie's baby be good at?

The question came out of nowhere, unsettling him even more. He didn't want to know anything about the baby and he grabbed onto the game as a focal point.

Moving, he positioned himself close to the boundary, expecting Richard to take advantage of Jack's inexperience. Both sides did that when the kids and women bowled, and the only exception to the rule was when they faced up to Auntie Karen. She'd played for the Australian Women's cricket team and not even the experienced cricketers among them could take many runs off her.

The thwack of willow against leather filled the air, along with calls of delight and frustration depending on which team people belonged to. Hamish kept his eyes firmly on bowler and batsman, following the arc of the red ball each time it was hit. Despite the change of bowler, Richard was still favouring the offside, which was nowhere near Hamish.

A flicker of movement in his peripheral vision made him turn his head. Georgie had leaned down and was picking up a water bottle. As she brought it up to her lips, she tilted her head back and took a long, slow drink.

His gaze stalled, fixed on her and totally mesmerised by the action. He took in the soft line of her jaw and the smooth expanse of her tanned and glowing olive skin, and suddenly an image of him trailing his tongue the full length of her neck and tasting her salty skin rocked through him.

He tore off his hat and ran his hand through his hair, before jamming the hat back on his head. What the hell was wrong with him? God, how many times had he seen her drink in seventeen years? Thousands? So why was he suddenly fascinated by it and getting hard in the process?

'Hamish!'

He heard Caleb and Ben roar his name and he turned to see a blur of red spinning down from high—the perfect catch. Only he wasn't remotely in position. As the ball plummeted earthwards, he ran hard and fast and launched himself at it, sliding along the ground with arms outstretched.

The ball hit the tips of his fingers, leaving no room to grip the leather, and the next moment it had trickled off his skin and landed with a puff of dust on the thin grass that grew out of reach of the sprinkler system.

He'd just dropped the perfect catch.

Furious with himself, he quickly swiped the ball up into his hand and threw it arrow straight back to Jack, who caught it, but not before Richard was home safe and had gained Omeo another four runs.

He trudged back to the pitch as the combined groan of the Jindi mob whipped him.

'What's up, bro?'

Caleb shook his head in disbelief while a crestfallen Jack stared at him, disappointment naked in his Pettigrew-blue eyes.

'Son, that's going down as the miss of the match,' Roy

said, slapping his back in bewilderment. 'I think you left your concentration back in India.'

Richard grinned. 'What was that you were saying about Omeo men being too easily distracted? I think we well and truly nuked that theory, mate.'

Hell. Had Richard noticed him staring at Georgie? Before Hamish could think of a deflecting reply, Opa said, 'That's the end of the twentieth over and after drinks it's Jindi's turn to bat.' He consulted Georgie. 'How many runs did Omeo make, dear?'

Georgie checked her notebook and looked up with a wide smile. 'One hundred and seven not out.'

Hamish felt the wrath of his family circling him again because with Richard not out, Omeo had just cemented a hard lead.

'Those are words every batsman likes to hear.' Richard stripped off his batting gloves and extended his hand to Georgie, his attention totally centred on her.

Hamish saw the moment his cousin's gaze flitted across the swell of her breasts and a buzzing noise filled his ears.

'I don't think we've met. I'm Richard Pettigrew, Roy and Denise's nephew.' He slid his palm against hers. 'Which part of the clan do you belong to?'

'Georgina and Hamish met at uni,' Caleb said.

'Really? He's done a wonderful job of keeping you hidden and all to himself over the years.' Richard glanced at Hamish. 'Cuz, you never mentioned you were going to be a father.'

Panic roared through him, closing his throat.

'You're very witty, Richard.' Georgie rolled her eyes with a playful glint.

Hamish held his breath, waiting for her to deny his paternity.

She tucked some stray hair behind her ear. 'But think about it. Can you seriously imagine Hamish wanting that sort of responsibility?'

Caleb snorted. 'You'd be hard pressed to know which one was the baby, hey, little brother?'

Neither Georgie nor Caleb were saying anything he didn't know to be true, but for some reason Hamish found it hard to give a good-natured smile at the cheap shots, even though Caleb's roasting was the perfect smokescreen to Georgie's decoy. His brothers had never made the connection about why he didn't trust himself to be a father. No one in the family ever had and he planned to keep it that way.

His throat relaxed, although a slightly bitter taste remained. 'You're just jealous I've got the freedom to take off at a moment's notice when—'

'Let alone commit to one woman for longer than half a year,' Ben added, slapping him on the back in a friendly tease. 'Now, if that did happen, it would be a Christmas miracle.'

Georgie's laugh sounded slightly strained. 'I rest my case.'

'Not to mention that fact that Georgie strikes me as far too sensible to have him,' Caleb said.

'I'm doing motherhood happily on my own, Richard,' Georgie said. 'Everything was going great until I hit a renovation problem and that's the reason I'm gatecrashing your family reunion. The Pettigrews are generously helping me by providing some temporary accommodation.'

Hamish nodded in agreement, keen to move the conversation as far away as possible from relationships, pregnancy and the baby. 'Georgie's house has asbestos and she had to move out fast. With it being close to Christmas—'

'There was no room at any of the inns?' Richard quipped, smiling down at Georgie again. 'That's appropriate, given the baby and the season. Now, after all that umpiring, can I get you a cool drink?'

'That's a great idea, Richard,' Denise said, rushing up to them. 'I've got everything from icy poles and oranges to tea and scones set up in the marquee, so come along.' She strode

off like the Pied Piper with a line of hot and thirsty cricketers following fast behind.

Georgie gripped Richard's proffered hand and rose out of
her chair with a smile. 'I'm feeling pretty hot and an icy pole
sounds wonderful, thank you.'

'You look serene but that's not to say that you're not *hot*.'
Richard hadn't let go of her hand.

Georgie giggled at the double entendre.

Hamish, having played her wingman enough times in
the past—including the night he'd introduced her to Luke—
instantly recognised it as her flirty tone. An odd green light
lit up behind his eyes.

It had him shooting out his hand and catching her elbow
while every part of him urged to distract her from Richard.
'Are you sure all that sugar is good for the baby?'

You're a moron. Why did you mention the baby?

Georgie's eyes shot open so wide he could have fallen
into them and her mouth pursed into a tight and disapproving line. He instantly remembered she hated being told what
to do as much as she craved to be independent.

'I *don't* have gestational diabetes, Hamish, so an icy pole
will be just fine.' She smiled at up Richard. 'Could you please
go and save me a red one before the kids eat them all? I'll be
there in just a minute.'

'Looking forward to it.'

Richard gave her a departing smile, but before he turned
and walked away he gave Hamish a direct look over Georgie's
head—one that was filled with a thousand questions.

CHAPTER SIX

'HAVE you lost your mind? I just set you up to be home free and now you do this?'

Hamish heard Georgie's hissed question and he thought perhaps he had lost his mind. Thinking about the baby was supposed to kill his sex drive, not raise a flag for Richard to zero in on.

He sucked in a breath that did nothing to steady him. 'Granted, it was a poor choice of words but it got your attention.'

'Oh and, "Georgie, can I talk to you for a moment?" wouldn't have?'

He ignored her sarcasm. 'It's important you know that Richard's a player.'

Georgie looked at him for a long, quiet moment and then she burst into gales of laughter. Rocking back and forth on her feet, tears ran down her cheeks and she pressed her hands against her sides as she gasped for breath.

Indignation poured through him. 'What's so funny?'

Hamish's offended tone dented Georgie's giggles and she blew out a couple of long breaths, trying to stifle the urge to keep laughing. His expression was a combination of hurt, confusion and misguided caring, but couldn't he see how ludicrous he was being?

'Haim, given how you live your life, isn't it slightly

hypocritical that you're warning me about a man who dates
a lot of women?'

A slither of hurt streaked through his eyes, making them
shimmer a deep blue. 'So sue me for trying to be a good
friend. I thought we looked out for each other?'

Only he'd *never* warned her about a man before. Usually
he was the one saying, '*Stop overthinking everything. Live
life and take a* chance,' so this behaviour totally mystified
her. All that aside, clearly her laughter had upset him and she
regretted that. 'I appreciate your concern for me, I do, but,
seriously, look at me.' She pointed to her tight belly that rose
out in front of her. 'I'm eight months pregnant and, player or
not, *no one* is going to be hitting on me.'

His head jerked up. 'Why do you always sell yourself
short?'

'I don't. I'm not.' The unusual light in his eyes made her
feel uncomfortable and she grabbed onto humour to try and
shift it. 'But we both know that I've always been the plain
one in this friendship and you're the pretty one. You've always been fighting off women and I've always been fighting to be noticed.'

'Don't be ridiculous.' He ran his hand jerkily through his
hair. 'Have I ever lied to you?'

The serious look in his eyes had her worried. 'No, of
course not.'

His expression seemed to be fighting itself as it ranged
from something close to distaste to the total opposite and
back again. He closed the gap between them and his warmth
coiled through her, carrying the familiar reassurance she'd
known for so long. It stroked her like the touch of a child's
soothing blankie. He moved again, dropping his head close
to her face, and his breath caressed her ear.

Soothing vanished—imploded by heat and need that tore
through her, stripping her leg muscles of all power and making her breath come in jerky runs.

'Believe me—' his usually mellow voice held an odd huskiness and then it dropped to an even deeper register '—some men find pregnant women incredibly sexy.'

Coherent thought fled. 'Are you sure?'

'Yeah. I know it for a fact.'

His lips were so close to hers that their energy vibrated the air between them, sending rafts of tingling pleasure pouring through her. All it would take was for her to move her head a millimetre and her lips would be cushioned against his and his taste of sunshine and salt would flood her. Then she'd trail her tongue along his bottom lip, branding him with her own heat before seeking entry to his mouth, where she'd lose herself in that hot, cavernous place she'd been thinking about non-stop for two days.

Just kiss him!

But she wasn't into emotional suicide, and French-kissing Hamish definitely came under that category.

He brushed a strand of hair behind her ear and the caress poured through her—pleasure backed with the torture that it was only a friendly gesture. For the briefest moment she thought she saw a flicker of heat in his eyes but then the shutters slammed down hard, quickly closing out every emotion until it was like looking into a sea fog.

'You don't realise it but you have a certain glow, George, which can be a magnet for men who are into the whole "pregnant is sexy" thing.'

She'd never thought of herself as sexy in her life, let alone now, and she didn't know whether to believe him or not. 'And you know this how?'

He shrugged. 'Guys talk. Not that I've never seen the attraction of pregnancy myself.'

One of his curls brushed her cheek, but it may as well have been a leather whip for the pain it inflicted. She swallowed and tried to make her voice sound normal so she could set things back on an even keel between them. 'And it would be too weird if you did with me, right?'

'Hell, yeah!' He stepped back abruptly, as if she was infectious, and the action, combined with his previous comment, gave clear and precise interpretation to the distaste she'd seen on his face earlier.

She hated it that everything inside her drooped. How stupid could she possibly be? He'd never found her attractive enough—even on the night so many years ago when they'd got close to making out, not even the assistance of too much wine had been enough to overrule the lack of chemistry he felt for her. He liked young and thin and she was anything but.

Add in she was pregnant with a baby he wanted nothing to do with, and why on earth had she even wondered if he found her attractive? Did she even want him to, when he didn't want the same things in life? Probably not.

What a mess. Pregnancy hormones confused everything, blurred boundaries and invented sexual chemistry. She couldn't believe how very close she'd been to totally embarrassing herself and making things even weirder between them than they already were. Rolling her shoulders back, she was determined not to give him a single hint about how hot and bothered he made her and how she was finding it increasingly hard to be relaxed around him.

'Hamish!'

They both turned, hastily stepping back from each other as Ben jogged over. For the first time in a long time Hamish wanted to hug his big brother. He needed this welcome interruption badly because for the first time in his long friendship with Georgie he'd just lied through his teeth to her. It had been that or crush his mouth hard against hers a mere fifty metres away from his entire extended family. A disaster of that magnitude didn't bear thinking about.

Neither Georgie nor his family were ever to know about

this insane attraction because a quick fling with Georgie was impossible, and he wasn't about to start playing happy families when he'd caused his own family a great deal of unhappiness.

'Mum's worried about Opa,' Ben said. 'Can you check him out?'

'Sure. What's the problem?'

His brother shrugged. 'Mum didn't say, but she looked worried so I said I'd find you.'

'Do you want me to go and get my bag?' Georgie offered, looking like she wanted an excuse to get away from him, and fast.

Given his behaviour over the past five minutes, he understood. 'That would be helpful, thank you.'

You're talking to Georgie, not your ER staff.

Her brows rose at his formal address. 'You're welcome, Dr Pettigrew.'

As Georgie walked away, he couldn't keep his eyes off her firm behind as the fabric of her dress moved across it, outlining its siren shape. She'd always worked out and she'd obviously kept up her exercise regime because despite her lush curves they were underpinned by toned muscle. Unlike some pregnant women, she didn't waddle at all.

Ben glanced at her retreating back and then back to him, his face full of enquiry. 'Everything okay?'

Hell, no. 'Yep.' He started walking quickly towards the marquee, immensely glad for the distraction of having something to concentrate on that made sense. Medicine made sense. Nothing about his reactions to Georgie made sense. The past five minutes had been a perfect example of that and it was doing his head in.

When he walked into the marquee, the cluster of people around his grandfather separated. 'So, Opa, what's up?'

His grandfather gave him a conspiratorial smile. 'Nothing

at all. Your mother's making a mountain out of a molehill and she's holding up the second half of the match.'

'Hamish, have you ever known your grandfather to sit out a cricket match?' Denise huffed, crossing her arms over her chest.

His mother had a point. 'Have you been feeling dizzy, Opa?'

'No, I'm as fit as a Mallee bull. Got the blood pressure of a sixty-year-old.'

Hamish knew plenty of sixty-year-olds who had hypertension, so the statement didn't reassure him. 'So why are you sitting out the match?'

'Can't an old man do what he feels like without having to give a reason?'

Hamish recognised the grumpy tone and knew he had to tread carefully because James Pettigrew had a stubborn streak a mile wide and had always shied away from fuss.

'Can I help?' Georgie lowered the emergency medical backpack to the ground.

'Why didn't my grandson carry that for you?' Opa asked, shooting Hamish a disapproving look. 'In my day, pregnant women were cosseted and taken care of. I gave your grandmother a cup of tea in bed every morning of our married life.'

Hamish stifled a sigh. 'Opa—'

'I'm quite capable of carrying it.' Georgie spoke over him. 'But thank you for your concern.' Her eyes twinkled at the old man as if they shared an understanding. 'We can argue out the sad lack of gallantry among modern men later if you like, although I'm tempted to think you only brought it up to move the focus away from yourself.'

His grandfather gave a sheepish grin. 'This young lady of yours, Hamish, is too clever by far.'

Hamish gritted his teeth. 'Opa, she's not my young lady, she's—'

'*Humph*! I'm not surprised, given the way you treat her.'

'James,' Georgie said quietly, but the warning tone was unmistakeable.

Unwise, Georgie. Hamish expected his grandfather to stand up and leave because he hated being told what to do as much as Georgie did, but with a jolt of surprise Hamish watched his grandfather bow to her unspoken request and reluctantly roll up the leg of his pants to reveal a white dressing on his shin. Georgie had managed to achieve what he and his mother had been trying to without success.

'It's just an infected mosquito bite,' Opa said, looking directly at Georgie. 'It's nothing to fuss about and I thought that keeping off my feet for a couple of days would help it heal.'

'That sounds like a sensible idea,' Georgie said, 'but seeing as you've got two doctors standing right here, it's probably worth us taking a peek.'

'James, would you prefer Georgina over Hamish?' Denise asked, giving Hamish an apologetic shrug.

Thanks, Mum. But he understood where she was coming from. The fact Opa had actually admitted the problem to Georgie was a miracle and the main aim of the exercise was appropriate treatment.

'She's definitely a prettier option.' Opa's rheumy eyes twinkled.

What the hell? Was every single Pettigrew male with a pulse hitting on her today?

Georgie snapped on some gloves, her face wreathed in a smile as she started to carefully remove the tape off Opa's thin skin. The gauze dressing didn't move. 'I've watched Hamish work his charm on women for years and now I know where he learned the art.'

Opa seemed to sit up straighter. 'But he can't seem to keep them. I kept a wonderful woman satisfied for fifty-one years.'

Hamish muttered a quiet oath and grabbed a bottle of saline, giving the top a vicious twist. 'This might be cold,

Opa.' He sloshed the saline over the gauze, wetting it so it would slide off easily.

'Fifty-one years?' Georgie sounded wistful. 'That's an amazing effort.' Her gloved fingers eased off the dressing and this time the gauze peeled back to reveal a deep and crusty wound with black edges.

Denise gasped.

Hamish swallowed his shock. 'Opa, this doesn't look like a mosquito bite.'

'I told you, it got infected.' His manner had become defensive again. 'What do you think, Georgina?'

Georgie's dark brows pulled down into a sharp V. 'When did you last change the dressing, James?'

'Two days ago.'

'Has the wound been getting bigger each time you change it?'

Opa's gaze shifted slightly. 'Perhaps.'

Hamish's brain started sorting through stored information. 'So it started off like a mozzie bite but it's been getting progressively bigger?'

James sighed. 'One night I forgot to light the citronella candles on the deck and I got a few bites. All of them went away except this one. It scabs up and then it just goes soggy again.'

Hamish picked up the ear thermometer and attached a new cone. 'I'm going to take your temperature.'

Georgie gave him an understanding nod and with her gloved fingers traced the necrotic edges of the wound. 'Does this hurt?'

Opa shook his head. 'There's never been any pain.'

The thermometer beeped. 'Thirty-six five. Opa, have you ever had a fever since you got the bite?'

'No.' His jaw tensed. 'I keep telling you I feel fine.'

Georgie raised her head and gave Opa a long, steady look

from her big, brown eyes—one that said, *Trust me*. 'How long ago did you get the mosquito bites, James?'

Opa's gaze flicked between her, Denise and Hamish and with a defeated sigh he said, 'A month ago.'

'Oh, Dad.' Denise sighed. 'Being independent is one thing but you should have told us or at least gone to see your doctor in Point Lonsdale.'

Georgie exchanged a quick look with Hamish and the next moment they were both saying, 'A painless, enlarging ulcer with no fever.'

She smiled at him—a smile of shared understanding. They both loved the buzz of working through the patient's history, combining it with the signs and symptoms and coming up with an answer. He realised he'd missed working with her.

'Opa, we think you've got a Bairnsdale ulcer. It's also known as the Daintree ulcer and the Buruli ulcer.'

'The flesh-eating bug?' Denise asked, horrified. 'Like you see in Africa? How on earth would he get that?'

Georgie pulled out a pathology swab and wanded it across the wound. 'In the last few years there have been quite a few cases of it on the Bellarine Peninsula, and Point Lonsdale is a hotspot for it. The bacterium's found in the soil there and it's been traced to being carried by mosquitoes.'

'I've read about it in the local paper.' Opa shook his head. 'I should have made the connection. Possums and koalas can get it too, as well as cats and dogs.'

Hamish gave his grandfather's shoulder a reassuring squeeze. 'Don't beat yourself up, although next time you have a wound that won't heal, you need to see a doctor earlier. Untreated, the toxins of this baby will eat through to the bone.'

Opa's face registered shock. 'So what's the treatment?'

Georgie slid the swab back into its container. 'We'll send this to Geelong for pathology just to be sure it's

Myobacterium ulcerans that's causing the problem, and we need to do some surgery on your leg.'

Denise stared at the large wound, concern clear on her face. 'Will he need a skin graft?'

Hamish shrugged. 'I'm an ER doctor, Mum, and I usually just refer this sort of thing on. George, you're the GP, what do you think?'

Georgie centred all her attention on Opa. 'James, this ulcer is borderline, but I think I can remove the dead tissue along with the recommended small margin of healthy tissue and that should leave just enough to avoid a skin graft. You'll also need to have antibiotic therapy. That said, I totally understand if you're more comfortable seeing a plastic surgeon in Geelong. Hamish can refer you to one of his colleagues.'

His grandfather laced his fingers in his lap. 'Have you treated something like this before?'

'I have.' Georgie placed a new dressing over the suppurating ulcer.

'Then I'd rather have you treat me here so I can continue to be part of the reunion.'

She rose and patted Opa's hand before turning to Hamish with a brisk look in her eye. 'Hamish, are you up for assisting me?'

She radiated a no-nonsense professionalism, and he relaxed under its touch, remembering how much fun they'd had working together before he'd left for the UK all those years ago. A time when everything had been easy between them as it had been up until she'd got pregnant. Working with her might just be the thing he needed to reset everything between them, to find normality again. To find his Georgie—his friend, the person he could always be completely himself with.

'Absolutely. I'll find Dad and ask him to put in a call to the hospital.'

'Excellent.' Georgie turned back to Opa. 'James, you still have time to change your mind. I won't be at all offended.'

Opa smiled at her. 'I won't be changing my mind, Georgina, but do you think we could finish umpiring the game before you put me under the knife? The Jindi boys have to answer the Omeo mob's challenge.'

Georgie grinned. 'Are you sure you're up for coping with bitter disappointment?'

'Hey, you should be on our side,' Hamish said, giving her a friendly prod with his hip.

'I'm impartial, remember?' She spun around laughing and her baby bump nudged him.

Before he could move backwards, he felt a firm kick against his stomach and the movement jagged through him like a jolt of electricity.

That's your baby.

Every muscle tensed so tightly they threatened to snap. The warm air in the marquee clogged his throat and his lungs cramped so rigidly that he could barely shift air in or out of them. Panic threaded through every cell of his body and he fought to keep the suffocating waves at bay.

It's not my baby. It's nothing to do with me. It's Georgie's baby. Georgie's. Baby.

'Are you all right, bro? You look a bit pale.'

Ben's voice sounded like it was coming from a long way away but he managed to croak out, 'Just a bit hot.'

'Drink this.'

Georgie shoved a cold can into his hand and he gulped it down fast, avoiding her gaze. No one could ever know it was so much more than heat.

'Come on, Hamish. Stop stalling.' Richard gripped his shoulder in friendly way. 'Omeo's got a cricket match to win.'

The good-natured taunting was a lifeline and he grabbed hold of it, letting it pull him away from all thoughts of

Georgie and the baby and take him back into his familiar world. His fingers pressed hard into the empty can, squishing it flat. 'In that case, prepare to be crushed.'

CHAPTER SEVEN

'Is YOUR baby going to be a Christmas baby?'

Georgie was surrounded by boys. Denise had co-opted her help with the craft activity that was part of the tradition of decorating the Weeroona Christmas tree. She'd happily accepted because it gave her something to do and kept her mind off the fact that her friendship with Hamish was struggling. Although he was doing a fair job of acting normally around her when his family was present, the most telling evidence that things weren't right between them was the fact that, unlike their first morning at Weeroona, he'd gone surfing at dawn twice without inviting her along.

Now, with the decorations made, Hamish's nephews and distant cousins were 'helping' decorate the fragrant *Pinus radiata*. As the noise level rose, Georgie remembered Hamish's comment that in his line of the family, no Pettigrew girls had been born in five generations. With a wry thought she realised that her decision not to find out the sex of the baby ahead of time was probably moot.

'No, Harry, my baby isn't going to be born until after Christmas.'

'Oh.' Caleb's six-year-old son sounded disappointed. 'Are you sure?'

Georgie steadied the ladder Harry was standing on so he

could hang his personalised decoration. 'Well, I'm pretty sure. Why do you want it to be born at Christmas?'

'Because we need a baby for the crib at Jindi.'

'Harry's right,' Denise said as she pointed the hot glue gun at another glass ornament. 'Jindi River always has carols on the beach on Christmas Eve and when we sing "Mary's Boy Child" and "Away in a Manger" we have a baby in the crib. This year there's a bit of a baby drought. Our youngest resident has just starting walking and would probably climb straight out.'

Georgie laughed. 'Sorry, at Christmas I'll still have three weeks to go so I doubt I'll be able to help.'

'Finished!' Harry jumped down.

'Can we go now?' Sammy asked, his concentration for the quiet indoor task fully exhausted. 'Uncle Richard said he'd take us tubing on the river when the tree was decorated.'

All the boys had hung their own personalised cherry-red Christmas ball—each with their name written in large gold glitter—on the tree, but it was hardly fully decorated and a box of older decorations lay untouched. Still, she sensed she'd have an uphill battle getting them to finish it and she was quite happy to listen to carols and complete the task herself.

'Okay, but first you must go to the laundry and put on sunscreen.'

'Richard's not going to let you in the water without your life jackets either so do it right first time, and then you won't have to come back to the house,' Denise added with a stern look at Tyler who tended to 'forget' the rules.

'Thanks!'

The thunder of departing feet against the polished boards rumbled around Georgie, making her smile. 'I can't believe one day I'm going to have one of those.'

Denise laughed. 'Boys are exhausting but lots of fun. Aren't you keen to get started? After all, thirty-seven weeks is considered term.' She reached out and rubbed Georgie's belly with a teasing look in her eye. 'Hey, Widget, you'd be helping out the Jindi carol service if you came early.'

'Please don't wish that on me, Denise.' Georgie gave a tight laugh. 'With the way everything's turned out I really need Widget to be two weeks late so I'm back in Melbourne.' *And not born in Jindi River surrounded by Pettigrews.*

Newborn babies tended to look like their fathers to promote bonding. Not that any father and child bonding was going to happen because this was her baby and hers alone. No, the reason she didn't want the baby born in Jindi River was because she didn't want Roy or Denise to see the baby and make any unwanted connections. Spending time with them over the past few days and really getting to know them better had been wonderful, and she didn't want to do anything to hurt them.

The grandmother smiled. 'The first lesson of motherhood, Georgina, is that babies come when they're ready, and the second is that children do things in their own way and in their own time. We have limited control and when they grow up we have none.'

She suddenly sighed and her usually smiling face was streaked with worry. 'Take my Hamish as an example. That boy was raised the same as his brothers and yet he's as unsettled as a rumbling volcano. I really don't think all this overseas work is good for him and he's certainly not been himself since he got back from India. You're close to him, Georgina. Do you think he's happy?'

The question was so unexpected and it caught her off guard. 'I suppose compared with Ben and Caleb, Hamish lives a less traditional life but that doesn't necessarily mean he's unhappy.'

Denise's lips pursed. 'Is "less traditional" code for saying he only dates girls who were born when he was in high school instead of mature women?'

She thought about Luke and Jonas. Both of them had

wanted her but only for as long as she had been prepared to live life their way. 'Believe me, not every man wants a partner, two kids, a mortgage and a dog, Denise.'

'Do you?'

Georgie's stomach sank and she tried a joke. 'No one wants a mortgage.'

'And your ex-boyfriend…' Denise tilted her head towards the baby bulge, obviously not willing to let the topic go. 'He's averse to commitment?'

Hating that she was lying by omission, Georgie pulled open the box of decorations and a plume of dust rose. She realised with a pang that it pretty much represented what had happened to her long-held dream for her life. 'I used donor sperm to get pregnant.'

Denise sat down, her face filled with bewilderment. 'I…I didn't realise.'

A traitorous thought sneaked in, pulling at Georgie's newly found confidence that this decision to have a baby on her own was the right one. It teetered on the realisation that a woman she admired might not agree with her. *That doesn't matter.* She felt her shoulders stiffen. 'I'm sorry you don't approve, but the baby and I will be just fine.'

'Darling girl, it's got nothing to do with disapproval and everything to do with me being sad for these thirty-something men like my Hamish who are missing out on so much by not ever experiencing the joys of a long-term relationship. He's great with kids when he lets himself relax, but it's like he's avoiding dating anyone who wants a future with him and I don't understand why. Unless…' She suddenly shook her head as if she'd changed her mind about what she was going to say.

Georgie thought of the parade of young, skinny girls Hamish had dated over the years. 'It's my experience that the guys don't quite see it as missing out on the joys of a long-term relationship, unless of course it's just…' Her voice cracked and she cleared her throat, thinking of Luke and Jonas. 'Unless it's just me they don't want.'

'Nonsense.' Denise jumped up, hugging her hard.

Georgie blinked fast, missing her mother desperately and trying not to sink into the understanding that flowed into her because Denise could never be part of her life after this short sojourn at Weeroona.

A moment later the older woman released her, and her eyes—the same bluer than blue as Hamish's—sparkled with cheeky fun. 'Don't get me wrong. I know how wonderful the heady wonder of lust and sex can be…' Her expression slowly sobered. 'But without an intellectual connection and shared experiences it all becomes very superficial and sex becomes an empty vessel.'

'What's an empty vessel?' Hamish asked, walking into the foyer, munching on an apple.

Georgie, still reeling from Denise's unexpected statement, got a second slam as lust ran headlong into surprise. Three days of sun and salt met with a shaft of sunlight, making Hamish's golden curls glow even brighter. This time she didn't even try to stop the tingle that wound through her and instead enjoyed it, knowing it was as close to sex as she was going to get with anyone for quite some time.

'Sex, dear,' Denise said with a perfectly straight face. 'Sex without an emotional connection.'

Hamish breathed in so fast that he inhaled apple and started coughing violently. He felt the slap of his mother's palm on his back.

'For heaven's sake, Hamish. You've been having sex since you were seventeen and pinched Ben's condoms.'

How did she know that? 'And I still don't want to talk about it with my mother,' he gasped, finally dislodging the apple.

Georgie's laughter circled him and he realised with a shot of alarm that his mother had been talking about sex to her.

Talking sex with a pregnant woman who glowed with sensuality. A woman carrying her grandchild.

The simmering panic that had become a part of him boiled over, adding to the permanent heat that flared every time he saw or thought of Georgie. It prickled and scratched him like a burr buried deep in a sock, making him irritable and cranky. 'Talking about sex in front of a Christmas tree is hardly appropriate.'

'Oh, I don't know,' Denise quipped. 'More babies are born in September in Australia than any other month so I think sex and Christmas are very much linked, don't you, Georgina?'

Georgie sucked in her lips as if she was trying hard to keep a straight face.

Damage control now. 'Mum, I think I hear Dad calling you.'

Denise rolled her eyes. 'I doubt that very much, dear, seeing as he's in town, getting supplies for the barbeque, but I take your badly disguised hint. I will leave and take my sex talk with me, but only if you agree to finish decorating the tree.'

'I'm fine to do it on my own, Denise,' Georgie said over quickly.

'I don't want you on the ladder, decorating the top of a fifteen-foot tree. We already have James in a wheelchair and we don't need you in one as well.'

Georgie's back straightened in the old familiar way it did when anyone dared suggest she might not be able to do something. 'I'm pregnant, not sick, and I'm perfectly capable of doing things on my own.'

After the debacle of the cricket match where his erratic behaviour and panic had almost blown all his chances of keeping his connection with Georgie's baby a secret, Hamish had spent the past two days avoiding spending any alone time with her. He'd mastered the art of not drawing attention to himself when they were in a group, although when Richard was around he made sure he was standing close by.

Right now, though, he had no group and no choice. If he refused to decorate the tree with Georgie, his mother would hound him until she found out the reason, which was a lot worse than coping with being alone with Georgie for an hour. Besides, he agreed with his mother about the ladder.

He nodded. 'Yes, you're fit and healthy, George, and no one's denying it, but Mum's right. Even though you're not huge, pregnancy upsets your centre of balance, so I'll do the ladder work.'

Georgie narrowed her eyes at him, but he could cope with a grumpy Georgie. More importantly, his mother was smiling in satisfaction, which meant she didn't suspect a thing. Something inside him relaxed. He'd finally found the right balance. His early-morning stress-reducing surf so he could cope with the whole disaster that was his life at the moment was paying off. His perceptive mother had no clue about him, Georgie and the baby.

'That's a big help, Hamish, thank you,' Denise said. 'I'll leave you two to get on with it and I'll go and bake some scones for afternoon tea.'

As Denise hurried away, Hamish avoided looking at Georgie's pregnant belly and asked, 'So, how do you want to do this?'

She tilted her head in thought. 'Your mum wanted these older ornaments on the tree so I guess, seeing as you've gone all Neanderthal man on me, I'll pass them up to you.'

'I was just keeping Mum off the scent.' *It's more than that.* Only he didn't want to admit anything so he hid behind doctor mode. 'I can't imagine you advising any pregnant patients to climb ladders.'

'Yes, but I'm sensible, remember.'

He laughed. 'You're not going to win this one, George, so you might as well give up now.' He picked over the ornaments in the box and shook his head. 'Wow, I made this cardboard and pasta bell when I was at Jindi kindy. I can't believe Mum has kept all this junk.'

'Family history, I guess. I plan to buy Widget a—' She stopped abruptly, a frown on her face. 'Sorry.'

'What for?'

'I know it freaks you out when I talk about the baby.'

'No, it doesn't.' The words shot out defensively fast as his brain screamed, *Liar*, and his body vividly recalled the baby's kick. A touch he'd been trying hard to forget.

She shook her head and a sad smile touched her lips. 'I've known you for seventeen years, Haim, and the only time you've remotely been yourself since we got here was when we operated on James. Even then you were more Dr Pettigrew, ER doctor, than my mate Hamish.' She sighed. 'I'm sorry that the most exciting thing in my life is getting in the way of our friendship. It wasn't meant to.'

She looked so forlorn that he felt a twinge of guilt. 'I know I said I didn't want blow-by-blow accounts about the pregnancy but seeing as you're staying here I also don't want you to feel you have to censor everything you say to me. I can cope with the occasional Widget reference.' *Really?* 'Just don't expect me to be involved in birth plans and definitely don't ask me about strollers or which nappies to use.'

'Deal.'

A wide smile crossed her face—a smile filled with warmth, friendship and utter relief—and he realised she'd been as tense as he had. A soft and reassuring feeling of familiarity filled him, and he recognised it as the sensation he'd always had when he was with Georgie—a sort of peaceful easiness that had been absent since he'd discovered she was pregnant. He breathed out a sigh of relief. All his surfing had paid off and he *finally* had everything under control.

Relaxing into the knowledge, he laughed. 'Okay, then,

let's get the last thirty-nine years of Pettigrew ornaments up and onto this tree.'

He positioned the ladder and they settled into a pattern of Georgie passing him the decorations one by one. The first few were decorations his parents had brought into their marriage from their own childhoods and he couldn't tell her much more about them than that, except they'd fascinated him as a kid.

He carefully pulled the pine needles through the string hanger on a star. 'Ben was ten when he made this out of drift-wood he found at the river entrance. It was probably the start of his career working with wood.'

'He was telling me about his hand-made chairs.'

'Yeah, they're pretty special, and Annie does an amazing job reed-weaving the seats. They've got a thriving business with most of their orders coming from Sydney and Melbourne.' Hamish hung three more decorations before he recognised and remembered the story of another one. He started laughing.

'What?'

Georgie looked up at him, her brown eyes filled with the warm glow of anticipation, and he realised how much he was enjoying sharing the stories.

'Caleb got into Mum's craft box and found a box of green and red sequins and a foam ball. Then he got Dad's super-glue.'

Georgie smiled. 'I think I can see where this is going.'

'He ended up with more sequins stuck to him than the ball and Mum went through a bottle of acetone removing them. At one point she threatened to leave them on and send him to school as a Christmas elf. Needless to say, Caleb lost interest in craftwork there and then and to this day he has a lot of respect for superglue.'

'I'd love to see a photo of that.'

'There's bound to be one somewhere. As you've seen, Mum's got photo frames everywhere.'

'On every flat surface.' A wistful expression crossed her face. 'You've got a lovely family, Haim.'

'They're all right in small doses.' He knew she was thinking about her parents so he shot her a full-wattage smile, wanting to halt any melancholy because he hated it when she was sad. 'What's next?'

Georgie passed up some cartoon characters he and Caleb had bought the year they'd holidayed on the Gold Coast, and he remembered how they'd run wild at theme parks for three days, having the time of their lives.

'Hey!' Georgie exclaimed, holding up a cherry-red ball with his name on it. 'This is just like the ones we made with the boys today.'

He accepted the bauble. 'Every Pettigrew kid ends up making one of these at some point during a ten-year reunion.' He pointed to the new baubles that had been made that day. 'This lot will be taken home by the owners to use on their own trees at future Christmases.'

She passed up Ben's, followed by Caleb's, and then she paused.

He glanced down as she gazed up, holding a fourth ball. 'Who's Aaron? One of your many relatives?'

His stomach pitched. He'd forgotten his mother had kept the ball and no way was he talking about Aaron. Talking made no difference to the facts—Aaron had died and he hadn't. He didn't want to tell the story about his beloved younger brother and have Georgie's eyes tainted by the look that would inevitably fill them, so he said, 'It must have got put in the wrong box.'

'Shall we hang it or give it to him? That's if he's here.'

His mouth was so dry his tongue stuck to the roof. 'We'll hang it and I'll let Mum know.'

The front door opened and it looked like a bunch of green

leaves was walking into the foyer until he recognised his father's legs and heard his muffled voice. 'Can you hang this next?'

'What is it?' Georgie asked, clearly bemused.

Roy held up the lantern-shaped foliage higher for a better view. 'It's mistletoe.'

'It doesn't look like that in the movies.'

Roy laughed. 'That northern-hemisphere stuff is tiny. We do it bigger and better down here, Georgina.'

Hamish rolled his eyes. 'What Dad's failed to mention is that it's a parasite that grows on eucalyptus trees.'

'It does the job, son, and I've never heard you complain. If I recall correctly, you've scored quite a few kisses from this parasite over the years.'

'That sounds about right,' Georgie teased, elbowing him playfully in the ribs.

Hamish opened his mouth to protest, wanting to tell her the real story, but his father started issuing instructions.

'Your mum wants it hung over the double doors that lead into the lounge room so I'll leave it with you because I'm setting up the citronella flares for the barbeque.' Roy thrust the mistletoe at him and hurried off.

'It's massive.' Georgie laughed. 'I think we'll need to trim it or there's no way anyone can avoid walking under it.'

Hamish shook his head. 'That's my parents' main aim. No one can escape without a kiss. Mind you, we can't complain too much as they're the biggest users of it, although Ben and Annie and Caleb and Erin aren't too shabby either.'

'Or you, by the sound of it.'

'Dad has the exaggeration gene. The last time I kissed a girl under mistletoe I was seventeen. I haven't brought a girl home for Christmas in…' He had to think.

'Not since Natasha,' Georgie said quietly.

He stared at her, stunned, realising she was right. 'Ah,

yeah. Not since Natasha.' Why had she remembered that? 'You've got a good memory.'

Georgie shrugged. 'So which long-legged blonde is the current woman of the moment?'

He positioned a tack in preparation for the mistletoe. 'I'm currently single.'

'Heavens, how are you coping?' Her eyes danced, along with her voice.

'Hell, Georgie, not you too.' He banged the tack in hard, suddenly sick and tired of the playboy jokes, especially as for the last nine months he hadn't hooked up with anyone. 'I get enough of that from my family without you joining in too.'

Contrition streaked across her face, followed quickly by a penetrating look. 'I'm sorry, I didn't realise it upset you.'

Neither had he and he tried to shrug it away. 'It's been a quiet year.'

'What do you mean?'

'I split up with Stephanie soon after you came to see me last year and I dated a couple of times, but I've pretty much been on my own since March.'

Her red bow mouth formed a perfect O of surprise. 'What's changed?'

'I don't know. It just seemed pointless starting something that would inevitably end.'

Her brows drew down slightly. 'A relationship doesn't have to end, Haim.'

'It does if the woman I date wants kids.'

Her hand fluttered over her belly. 'I look at your family and I don't understand why you're the one son who doesn't want what your parents and brothers have. Why are you so adamant about not wanting children?'

His heart rate jumped into the fast zone and he felt unsteady on the ladder. *Because I might make a massive mistake, like I did with Aaron.* He ducked the truth. 'I don't want that sort of tied-down, in-your-face responsibility.' He forced a grin at her. 'I'm a free spirit, George, you know that.'

Her big brown eyes held his gaze but their expression was suddenly sceptical. 'So find a career-woman who doesn't want a family. They're out there.'

He put the hammer down and then hung the leaves, determined to change the subject. 'How's that?'

'It's not centred.'

'Yes, it is.'

She shook her head. 'It's more to the right, which means people could sneak through and avoid your parents' evil plan.'

He was unconvinced and went and stood under it. 'You try walking through.'

She shook her head. 'I'm hardly the best test as I'm wider than every other person here.'

He grinned. 'You're forgetting Uncle Alec twice removed. I've been trying to work the words "diabetes test" into every conversation I have with him. You're positively skinny compared to him.'

She gave a snort of laugher. 'I'm going to take that as a compliment of sorts. Okay, here goes.' She started walking through the doorway.

'See.' He put his hand on her arm to stop her before she'd passed through completely and he pointed to the mistletoe, which not only hung over her baby bump but over her head. 'Everyone who walks in gets caught.'

'That *is* a wicked plan.' Her words slipped out on a whisper and her eyes darkened to the colour of rich, hot, chocolate sauce. She looked sultry, luminous and incredibly sexy. Tilting her chin slightly, she fixed her now clear gaze on his.

His breath caught as he recognised desire shining in their depths as clearly as if it was written in ink.

She wanted him.

Nine months of abstinence exploded.

Don't do it.

But he was tired of resisting and he was deaf to all reason. Slowly, he raised his hand to her mouth, tracing the plump and moist redness of her bottom lip with his finger. 'It's beyond wicked.'

She shivered under his touch and her tongue flicked out, caressing the tip of his finger. Then her lips moved, closing around it.

The gentle suction made his head spin. He wasn't inexperienced and yet Georgie's mouth sucking at his finger was the most erotic thing that had ever happened to him. He ached with need and every part of him wanted to touch her. He raised his other hand to her jaw, tracing her cheekbone with the pad of his thumb, marvelling at how silky soft her skin felt against his rougher palm.

She sighed—an almost purring sound—and it was the only invitation he needed. His finger fell from her lips and he lowered his mouth over hers, kissing her with a gentle, questioning sweep of his lips. *Do you really want this, Georgie?*

Her hands flew to his hair, gripping his head and angling it so that his mouth pressed hard against hers. From that moment he was lost. Gentle vanished under her urgent touch and desire took over, releasing days of repressed agony. Her mouth was hot and wet and he couldn't get enough of it. She tasted of Christmas spices, vanilla and a hint of toothpaste—a sweet and sexy combination that sprang his body into a frenzy.

He wanted it all. He wanted to inhale her, consume her, brand her and take her as his. He buried his fingers in her hair, loving the way the long, smooth strands slid like water through his fingers.

A soft moan left her lips and he moved his exploration along her jaw. He nibbled her ear and she sagged against him. Instead of the touch freaking him out like last time, the tight feel of her belly pressing into him only aroused him more, and as her head fell back, exposing her neck, he nuzzled his face into the curve of her neck and pressed kisses to her skin, slowly moving downwards until his tongue slipped into the soft dip at the top of her wondrous breasts. He was home.

'What are you doing?'

Like being hit by a taser, Hamish jerked back at the sound of a child's voice and heard Georgie's shocked gasp. Somehow he managed to get his voice to work. 'Testing the mistletoe, Rupe.'

The four-year-old boy looked confused. 'I thought Nana said people kissed under mistletoe.'

'They do, buddy.' He turned and ruffled his nephew's hair.

'Daddy doesn't kiss Mummy like that,' he said dubiously.

'Hamish was looking at my pendant,' Georgie said hurriedly as she backed farther away from him, her expression soft, stunned and tinged with the same need that throbbed through him.

Her mouth twitched in a wry smile but he couldn't tell if she was relieved at Rupert's interruption or not. The kid's timing totally sucked, although making out with Georgie within sight of Weeroona's busy front door was not on his list of most sensible decisions.

Just lately, nothing to do with his feelings for Georgie was sensible. He probably should be thanking Rupert, except that every part of him wanted to grab her hand, run her up the wide staircase to his room and bolt the door behind them.

Georgie bent down to Rupert's eye level and picked up her pendant, going with the story she'd just told. 'See, it's a pretty opal.'

Rupert reached out, his little fingers tracing the shot of pink that wound through the sea-blue. Hamish wished he was in Rupe's place.

'Why aren't you with the other boys?' Georgie asked.

His bottom lip wobbled. 'They said I was too little.'

'Ah.' Hamish's blood had finally reached his brain and he remembered being told the same thing. He remembered telling Aaron that a couple of times too and then regretting it so very much when his younger brother no longer tagged after him.

As much as he'd wanted to race Georgie somewhere, he could tell by the look on her face that it wasn't going to happen. Added to that, the look on Rupert's face made him want to be a good uncle to his young nephew. He bent down. 'Tell you what, Rupe, I'll string the lights on the tree and down the banisters and you can be in charge of turning them on. How does that sound?'

Rupert's eyes grew as round as saucers. 'That's a big-boy job.'

Hamish grinned, loving the feeling that came with it. 'It sure is, and it's something you can tell your big brothers about. Something they didn't get to do.'

'Your Uncle Hamish is a clever man.' Georgie caught his eye and her smile lost its wryness, expanding into one of shared understanding.

Something shifted inside him and he didn't know why. It wasn't like they'd never agreed on something before and it certainly wasn't the first time she'd told him he was clever, although her praise was usually connected with his medical abilities.

'Georgie will take a photo of you so you can show everyone.' He reached out his hand, catching Georgie's to help her rise to her feet and to make sure she didn't bolt. Being a kind and loving uncle was one thing, but the moment the tree was lit and they'd found a supervising adult for Rupert, he intended to take her somewhere private and finish that kiss.

CHAPTER EIGHT

THAT kiss. Georgie had relived it a thousand times—going hot and cold in the process—but no matter which angle she came at it, she couldn't get past the fact she'd never experienced a kiss like it. A kiss that had had her losing track of time and place, and risking everything she and Hamish had worked so hard to keep secret. What if an adult Pettigrew had walked in on them? Her mouth dried at the thought. It would have come under the banner of cataclysmic disaster and it didn't bear thinking about.

The kiss, on the other hand, was seared into her brain, and she thought about it constantly. From the moment Hamish's finger had touched her lips she'd dumped caution, wanting and needing his touch like an addict needed his or her next hit. Her cheeks burned at the memory of how she'd literally thrown herself at him but her body tingled at the recollection of how wonderful it had felt to be in his arms and inhaling his scent, taste and touch. And he'd kissed her back.

Despite days of aghast looks from him and long moments of strained silence when she'd known he'd wished her anywhere but here at Weeroona, he'd kissed her back and then some. At the time it felt so right but now, a few hours later when she'd had time to think, she was more confused than ever and she needed to talk to him about it. Finding the time, however, was the challenge. The moment Rupert had flicked the switch to light up the tree—and his eyes had lit up almost as brightly—Hamish had been swept up by his family to play in a tennis tournament. She'd never met a family so into their sport.

Georgie had been invited to watch but as her body was already buzzing from the kiss, she didn't need to add the visual overload of watching an athletic Hamish chase a green ball around the court. She'd used the time to grab a quick rest but although her body had been inactive, her mind had never stilled. After fifty minutes she'd given up and she was now outside, planning to read by the pool.

'Hey, Georgie, how are things?' Richard called out as he walked towards her with a tennis racquet slung casually over his shoulder.

Messy and muddled. 'Is the tennis finished already?' She couldn't help peering into the distance toward the courts to see if she could glimpse Hamish.

Richard gave a self-deprecating shrug. 'I'm more of a cricketer than a tennis player and I missed your lucky presence.'

His easy flirting made her laugh. 'Me being there watching has no impact on your game whatsoever.'

His green eyes crinkled at the edges. 'But it does on Hamish. Without you on the sidelines he had his concentration back and he whipped me six-two.'

She heard the tightness in her laugh as her entire body went on full alert. *Distract and deter.* 'I doubt that had anything to do with me and everything to do with the fact that Hamish is more of a tennis player than a cricketer.' The baby kicked her and she suddenly had an idea that might help sidetrack Richard from making unwanted associations between her and Hamish.

'Richard, my car's in Geelong and I've arranged a prenatal appointment there tomorrow rather than going all the way back to Melbourne. I was wondering if you could drive me to the bus stop at Jindi at eight?'

'I'll do better than that. I'll drive you to Geelong.'

Georgie hated being beholden to anyone and she'd already notched up more debt than she could ever repay to the Pettigrews. 'That's really kind of you, but driving to Geelong will shoot your entire day. Really, the bus is fine.'

He shook his head, his expression adamant. 'I've got Christmas shopping I need to do so it's no problem at all. We can leave straight after breakfast.'

The thought of bypassing the stop-start bus ride as the bus pulled in and out of every coastal town and hamlet was very tempting. 'Are you sure it's not putting you out?'

'I'm absolutely certain it's not putting me out in the least. Tell you what, to put your mind at rest, if you have time after your appointment, you can give me some present suggestions for the hard-to-buy-for people and we'll call it even. I'll enjoy having some company in the car and you can fill me in on your house and baby plans.'

She shook her head quickly. 'I wouldn't dare bore you by doing that.'

'It won't bore me at all.' A quizzical smile darted across his face. 'I imagine that your head's full of it as that one of life's most momentous events is about to happen to you.'

A dull pain jabbed her under the ribs. Richard had just given voice to exactly how she was feeling. With Hamish, she censored every word about the baby and as lovely as Roy and Denise were, she was so busy being careful not to give anything away that she'd hardly talked about Widget to them either. All in all, it was like she'd been sublimating part of her—a part she should be enjoying.

Like a pressure valve being released, she suddenly felt a lot lighter. 'So you're truly up for an in-depth discussion on stroller suspension and three-pack kitchen benches?'

'I chose granite for my renovation and any talk about things with wheels, I'm so there.'

For a moment his easy manner reminded her exactly of how she and Hamish had once been with each other and it rammed home how much she missed it.

'Help! I need help!'

Georgie spun round toward the sound of an anguished voice. An older woman she didn't recognise was running up the long drive, waving her arms frantically. She spoke automatically, the doctor in her coming to the fore. 'Richard, get Hamish. Now.'

'I'm on it.' Richard ran.

'Jenny?' Denise rushed out of the back door, her face pale and drawn with worry. 'What's wrong?'

'It's Ken. He was… We need…' Jenny was panting so hard that Georgie was worried she was going to collapse. 'Hamish. Ken needs a doctor.'

'I'm a doctor.' Georgie laid her hand on the woman's arm. 'And Hamish is on his way. Where's Ken?'

But the woman had no spare breath to answer her.

'They live on the next property,' Denise told her as Hamish rushed up with the medical kit. 'But that's at least four hundred metres away. You'll need to take the quad bike.'

Georgie gave a vote of thanks she was carrying the baby quite compactly as she scrambled onto the wide bike seat and clicked the helmet's chin strap closed.

'Jenny.' Hamish's tone made the woman's head snap up and her eyes focus. 'Tell us exactly where he is.'

'Near the Creamery Lane gate. He's…he's pinned underneath a eucalypt limb.' Jenny's voice cracked. 'Oh, God, please let him be all right.'

Hamish exchanged a gulping look with Georgie, and she knew exactly how he was feeling. The human body didn't cope at all well with being crushed. She saw the moment in his eyes when his dread receded and the ER doctor took over.

'Mum, ring triple 0 and tell Dad to bring the chainsaw.' The quad-bike engine roared into life as he slammed his helmet on his head. 'Hang on, George.'

Hamish steered the sturdy, cross-country vehicle down the back of the block through a paddock of sheep and Georgie's hands tightened around his waist as her thighs gripped the wide black seat. As Hamish criss-crossed, avoiding the grassy tussocks, she kept her gaze flitting one hundred and eighty degrees, not wanting to miss their patient.

After about four excruciating minutes she finally saw something—a massive log on the ground at the bottom of a steep gully.

She tapped Hamish's shoulder and yelled, 'There.'

He swung around, his face pale. 'Get off.'

'No, you're going to need me.'

'The baby—'

'Will be fine. I'm fit and healthy and a bit of bouncing isn't going to hurt.' Had it been anyone else behind the wheel she might have thought twice, but she trusted Hamish implicitly and right now a possibly dying man needed her expertise. She made herself smile as if she was more confident than she really felt. 'Come on, hurry up, but in the safest way possible.'

He didn't look happy but she saw the moment he capitulated. 'You *must* lean in close and wrap your arms tightly around my waist.'

He turned the bike commencing a slow zig-zag trajectory down the gully and a couple of heart-stopping moments later they were on flat ground and next to the tree. The second he killed the engine, Georgie yelled, 'Ken.'

Hamish jumped off the bike, grabbing the emergency kit and heading toward the faint call of 'Here'.

It took Georgie slightly longer to dismount and, giving thanks that she'd kept fit, she managed to cross the short distance quickly just as Hamish was unzipping the medical kit.

Ken, who looked to be in his sixties, was pinned from his

left shoulder to his right knee, crushed by an enormous log. A discarded chainsaw lay on the ground next to a heap of rope.

He glanced between them. 'Get me out, please.'

Georgie immediately started priming IV tubing. 'We will, but first we have to establish a fluid line because when we remove the pressure of the log your blood pressure can drop. This way we can counter that.'

Hopefully counter that. There was a huge risk Ken could bleed to death in front of them.

'Ken, this is Georgina,' Hamish said, sliding his hand under the log to see if there were any spaces at all that would allow him to attach Ken to the portable monitor and defibrillator. 'She's a doctor and a very good friend of mine. We met at med school.'

Ken's pain-and-fear-filled eyes fixed on her as if she was a lifeline in a rough sea. 'You're pregnant. First baby?'

Georgie nodded, understanding his need to talk. Scared patients could react in a variety of ways and Ken was taking the 'everything is normal' approach rather than thinking about the fact he might die.

'Yes, due in January.'

'My wife gave me five wonderful children.'

'Five? Wow. Right now I can't see past one.' She managed to hang the IV bag on a low branch of the tree.

'The moment they smile at you you're a goner.' His voice wavered but he kept talking as if stopping was his greatest fear. 'Jenny was like you, working right up to the birth. Some women are born to pregnancy and others struggle.' He paused for breath. 'Looks like she's a natural, eh, Hamish?'

Georgie expected Hamish to ignore the comment as it was about pregnancy and the baby—his two least favourite subjects—but he nodded at Ken with a knowing smile. 'Yep, she's got the glow.'

His outback-blue eyes filled with a similar look to that he'd given her under the mistletoe. It both thrilled and disconcerted her, but she had no time to think about it. Sliding a tourniquet over Ken's arm, she clicked and tightened it. 'This needle might sting.'

The older man grimaced. 'Sweetheart, that's the least of my problems.'

And it was.

Hamish's frown burrowed crevicelike into his brow, the way it always did when he was extremely stressed, and he had every reason to be. 'Run the Hartmann's in full bore and insert a second line. His BP's fair but...'

And she knew exactly what he meant. From shattered bones and ribs to a host of possible internal injuries, including the possibility of a ruptured spleen and a lacerated liver, the biggest risk would come when they pulled Ken free.

'Respiration's rapid.' Hamish pulled his stethoscope out from under the log. 'Heart rate eighty-five. Ken, where does it hurt?'

'Everywhere, mate.'

'Anywhere hurt more than somewhere else?'

'My arm and chest.'

'How's the breathing.'

'Okay.'

Hamish connected the mask and tubing to the black-and-white portable oxygen cylinder and adjusted the mask over Ken's face by pulling the green elastic tight. 'This will help. Dad's on his way so we can get this log off you and that's going to be the most dangerous part of the day.'

Terror flared in Ken's eyes but he still tried for a joke. 'Yeah, let's hope he doesn't hold a grudge about losing the lawn-bowling championship to me.'

Georgie squeezed Ken's hand. 'Ken, there's a big chance you might lose consciousness when the log comes off so we'll give you a minute with Jenny before we do anything.'

'Hell, now you're scaring me.' He sucked in a breath. 'I'm tough as old boots, love.'

'That you are,' Hamish said quietly, 'but Jenny isn't.'

'Yeah. Still, she's gonna yell at me soon enough and call me a stupid old fool, and for once I'm going to agree with her. One minute I was harnessed in the tree and the next minute I was down here.'

Georgie shone her torch in his eyes and checked his pupils. 'Did you black out?'

He shook his head. 'Don't think so.'

The roar of an engine made them turn, and Roy's battered ute came barrelling up the track, a plume of dust in its wake. Ben and Caleb jumped out of the tray with the chainsaw and Roy, Denise and Jenny spilled out of the cab. Jenny raced over, and Hamish explained what was going to happen and the possibilities. The woman swayed and Georgie caught her elbow to steady her.

She and Hamish withdrew to give the couple a few precious moments of privacy and Hamish spoke with his father and brothers about cutting the log. 'Plan A is we use both chainsaws and cut at either end so we can reduce the weight without risking cutting too close to Ken. Then we have six people—'

'Seven,' Georgie interjected.

'You are not lifting that log.'

She blinked in surprise at his intransigent and protective tone and opened her mouth to object when Denise said, 'Hamish is absolutely right, Georgina.'

'You're needed with Ken, Georgie, in case he goes into cardiac arrest,' Hamish instructed, before showing Ben and Caleb where they were to cut. 'Georgie and I are going to have our hands full so, Mum, you need to look after Jenny, and, Dad, you need to go and meet the ambulance.'

'Erin's doing that,' Caleb said.

'Great. Thanks.' Hamish gave them a look she'd seen him give to his triage team many times before. 'If in the next hour I yell at any of you, it's not personal.'

Ben's hand squeezed Hamish's shoulder in perfect understanding. 'Bro, we're just thankful you're here. You too, Georgie.'

She nodded, knowing that Ben meant he was glad to have her here as a doctor, but all the rational thoughts in the world didn't stop a silly wave of loneliness that she didn't have a family who could say something like that to her. That was why she was starting her own family with her own baby who'd love her and care for her.

A baby who's half-Pettigrew.

No. This baby was hers. They would be a team of two—their own family unit because neither of them belonged with the Pettigrews. Her way was the best way. By not involving anyone else, there was no risk of being left or abandoned.

As the chainsaws roared into life, Georgie returned to their patient. 'It's time, Jenny.'

The older woman nodded and she kissed Ken's forehead. 'I'll be over there, close by. I love you, you old fool, so just you remember that.'

'I love you more, Jen.'

The gruffly spoken words made Georgie's throat tighten and she wondered what it would be like to live a life with a man who loved her so completely. She doubted she'd ever know.

Denise arrived and gently took Jenny by the arm, and as the women walked away Georgie knelt down beside Ken.

'I'm going to put your earmuffs back on your ears to muffle the noise.' Mostly it was to shield him from what the noise represented.

Ken just nodded, so she put the muffs in place and then rechecked his vital signs. Thankfully they were holding, but she knew this was just the calm before the storm.

After what seemed like an eternity, the chainsaws fell silent.

'On my count,' Hamish yelled.

'This is it, Ken.' Georgie opened the second IV to full tilt.

'Good luck with that baby,' Ken said.

'One, two, three.'

The log started to move slowly, with the four Pettigrew men working as a team to save their neighbour, but Georgie didn't have any time to be watching them because her total attention was fixed fully on Ken. His blood pressure was holding but it was early days and she held her breath. She changed IV bags and rechecked his pressure. It had fallen slightly. 'Ken, how are you going?'

His head rolled towards her, his expression cloudy. 'Feel funny.'

'Stay with me, Ken.' She heard the urgency in her voice and wished she had an operating theatre a moment away, but she didn't and Ken's life force was probably being pumped into his belly right this minute. She squeezed the IV bags and prayed for the ambulance with its new supplies.

'How's he going?' Hamish was beside her.

'BP's eighty on not much. I've got the adrenaline drawn up.'

'Eighty I can deal with.' Hamish looked optimistic for the first time since arriving on the scene. 'Let's hope it's the new post-log pressure.'

Ken's eyes rolled back.

Hamish swore. The monitor squealed. Jenny screamed.

'Commencing CPR.'

Georgie exchanged a look with Hamish and prayed there was enough circulating volume left in Ken's veins for his heart to pump.

CHAPTER NINE

HAMISH smiled as he recalled the hotel receptionist's expression when he and Georgie had checked in wearing scrubs and she'd asked if they'd had fun at a fancy-dress party.

If only.

By the time they'd arrived at the hospital with Ken, their clothes had been streaked with blood and dirt, and scrubs had seemed the best option so as not to freak people out. Tomorrow he'd call by his fume-laden house and grab some fresh clothes for both of them before they drove back to Jindi.

The past six hours had been really tough and there'd been too many moments when he'd thought Ken would die in front of them. He'd had to work hard at keeping memories at bay of another trauma not far from the same spot. At least this time he'd known what to do. He hadn't had to stand by and watch helplessly. He'd poured every ounce of emergency medicine knowledge and experience into treating Ken and somehow, against the odds, he and Georgie had managed to keep him alive long enough to get him to the operating theatre. Two surgeons had done an amazing job and now Ken was in the ICU in a critical condition and filled with tubes and donor blood, but thankfully he was alive. He couldn't deny to himself what a great team he and Georgie made.

Having made sure Jenny was being looked after by her adult children, there'd been nothing left for either Georgie or him to do. Given the late hour and the distance by road to Jindi River, they were staying the night in Geelong. The plush carpet of the hotel room was soft under his feet as he sipped a glass of Leura Park pinot noir and stared out at the lights across the bay. He could hear the emergency helicopter coming in to land again and knew it was another busy night for the staff at the hospital.

'Sorry I took so long. Bathroom's all yours.' Georgie appeared in the room straight from the shower. Her hair was damp and tousled, her face glowed, and her body was wrapped in a thick, plush, towelling robe.

His gaze stuck on the white sash tied under her round belly. *That's your baby.* He gulped his wine. This double hotel room was the only one available and apparently that had only been due to a last-minute cancellation.

He and Georgie alone in a hotel room together.

He took another slug of his drink, ignoring the horror of his internal wine buff that he wasn't savouring the complex flavours. Eight hours ago on the tail of *that* kiss, he would have thought that the two of them here together would be the perfect venue for a follow up. Now he wasn't so sure.

Downstairs at Reception, when they'd been told about the room situation, Georgie had given a very tight laugh and joked about the last time they'd shared a room years ago at a conference. He suddenly recalled feeling oddly unsettled that night and how he'd deliberately gone to the bar after dinner rather than coming straight back to their room. There he'd met Ellen, and Georgie had ended up with the room all to herself.

He rubbed the bridge of his nose. In his experience, the evoking of a memory about a past girlfriend wasn't indicative of a woman wanting to revisit a kiss.

He tried a smile. 'Thanks, but I grabbed a quick shower at the hospital when I got changed.' He held up his wine glass.

'Do you want something? They've got sparkling mineral water or ginger beer.'

'Mineral water would be nice, thanks.'

She joined him at the window, and the coconut and lime scent of her hair reminded him of hot tropical nights. Immediately, an image of Georgie standing pregnant and proud in a bikini flooded him, and he spilled the water he was pouring. 'Damn it.'

Georgie grabbed some tissues and sopped up the mess. 'You're really strung out about Ken, aren't you? Remember, it was you and all your experience who saved his life.'

He accepted Georgie's unintentional rescue rope, acknowledging there was truth to it. 'He's Dad's best mate, and I've known him all my life.'

'Working on a family friend is very different from treating someone you don't know.' Thoughtfulness infused her voice—the sort of understanding that could only come from someone who'd been in a similar situation.

He let it flow around him in supportive rings. Georgie had always been able to read him in a way no one else could.

'Yeah, it's hugely different.' The feelings of helplessness he thought he'd vanquished rose again, and he breathed in against them. 'Ken and Jenny helped our family get through a very tough time. After all they've done for us, there was no way I was letting him go. I owed him that.'

Her brown eyes filled with an almost wistful look. 'Growing up in a small town must be incredibly supportive.'

Memories crowded him. 'Yes and no. It can be stifling sometimes when they know everything about you and look at you differently as a result.'

She wriggled her nose. 'But surely that would just be the gossips. Good friends are always there for you.'

Her face shone with caring, the way it often did when she looked at him, and it hit him like a thump to the chest. Apart from his family, he could hardly count on one hand another person who cared for him so much. Given everything he'd been through that day, he suddenly he wanted to tell her about Aaron. He needed to. He no longer wanted to have that secret between them.

'I'm not the youngest in my family, Georgie. I have—' He corrected himself, 'I had a younger brother. Aaron. He died when I was twelve.'

She looked surprised and her hand slid into his as if she knew instinctively that the story wasn't going to be easy to tell. 'Aaron of the Christmas bauble?'

He nodded. 'That's him. I was three when he was born and after being bossed around by two older brothers I was finally one myself. In fact, Mum promoted the whole big-brother thing to me as a way of easing my transition from being the baby of the family to the notorious third.'

She smiled softly. 'Denise is a wise woman.'

'Very true, only don't tell her I said that or she'll remind me of my words at the most inopportune times.' He refilled his wine glass. 'Unlike with Ben and Caleb, I got on really well with Aaron. We were pretty much inseparable out of school and we'd spend hours playing cricket and mucking about in an old tinnie boat on the dam. In total contrast to my other brothers, Aaron pretty much hung on my every word and most times would happily do whatever I suggested. He was my best mate, and I'd be lying if I didn't get off on the ego trip of a kid who looked up to me and expected me to know stuff.'

He watched a group of people spill out from the French restaurant across the road. Their disparate ages and the time of year hinted that they'd been at a work Christmas party. A young group linked arms and walked rowdily up the street in the direction of the nightclub as the older crew hopped into waiting taxis.

Georgie squeezed his hand. 'It all sounds pretty special. You had some hero-worship and a best buddy.'

'I did.' He forced himself to turn away from the window and gazed down at her, steeling himself for the moment the expression in her eyes would change but risking it anyway. 'Only I let it get out of control and I lost it all. Aaron died because I did the wrong thing.'

She kept her gaze on his face, her expression filled only with concern for him, and waited silently, as if she knew that he had to tell the story in his own way.

He swallowed against a tight throat, sideswiped by the raft of feelings that her understanding stirred up in him. He stared at her hand resting in his.

'The day Aaron died was a hot one. It was the summer before I started high school. Ben and Caleb were away at Country Week for cricket, and Aaron and I were enjoying not being bossed about.

'Mum had packed us a picnic and we'd gone to the dam, but after an hour of swimming we were looking for something else to do. Aaron had a new bike and he wanted to try it out on the Creamery Lane hill. Ben and Caleb had taught me the tricks and skills for riding the gravel and now it was my turn to pass the knowledge on.'

He raised his gaze to hers, needing to see her face. 'The deal was that I'd go first and he'd follow, but in one of his few rebellious moments he took off before me.' His chest burned as the memory crashed through him. 'I yelled at him to stop but he just raised his hand in a wave. I jumped on my bike but he was too far ahead for me to catch him up. Three-quarters of the way down the hill he lost control of the bike, skidded around the blind turn at the bottom of the hill and straight into an oncoming milk tanker.'

Her hand gripped his hard. 'Oh, God, Haim. How awful for you, for him, for everyone. I'm so sorry.'

He heard her distress for him but he didn't respond because he wasn't finished and if he stopped now he'd never get it out. 'The tanker driver did CPR until the paramedics arrived and Aaron was airlifted to Melbourne. Everyone worked so hard to try and save him and none of them wanted to let him go, but now after years of medicine I know he would have died instantly.'

He rubbed the back of his neck as if it might help the unforgiving ache inside him. 'I should *never* have let him go down that hill. My adoring little brother, my best mate, vanished from our lives, leaving a massive hole, and it was all my fault.'

'No, Hamish, it was an accident.'

Her soft words had steel behind them but he shook his head. 'I was the responsible older brother. I should have known he didn't have enough experience on his new bike and I should have said *no*. I should have waited a few more months, but I ignored all that because he begged me and I wanted to be the favourite brother.'

Her mouth firmed into a resolute line. 'You were twelve, Hamish. A kid yourself, and you tried to stop him.'

A thousand regrets burned behind his eyes. 'And it was the one time he didn't listen. I'll never forget the shock and grief I put on my parents' faces.'

She shook her head almost violently. 'Hamish, your parents love you. I see it in every word and action. They don't blame you.'

And one tiny part of him knew she spoke the truth but a much bigger part carried the culpability.

Her eyes suddenly widened. 'This is why you don't want children, isn't it? You don't trust yourself. Oh, Haim, you lost more than a brother that day.' Her whispered words combined with her gaze, which was far too perceptive for comfort.

He shook his head. 'I failed at being responsible. Everyone knows that and you can't argue it because no one in the family has expected anything of me since.'

She wrinkled her nose. 'I think that's how you saw it

through your grief and trauma when you were twelve and you've let it play out that way ever since.'

Her words rubbed at him like an ill-fitting boot. 'No, that isn't the case at all. The foundations of our family were so badly shaken and they had to resettle around an empty space.'

Her head tilted and her intelligent gaze bored into him. 'I totally understand how it happened but you're thirty-five now, Haim, and you don't have to be ruled by this any more. You're allowed to want a family. You don't have to play the role of the Pettigrew son who never grew up. You're allowed to be responsible outside work.'

Her words nipped at the edges of the mess of emotions he'd been ignoring for years—emotions he intended to keep ignoring. He'd had enough of talking about this and he went for humour. 'You say that and yet you've met my older brothers, Ben and Caleb.'

Her lips twitched in a half-smile before she asked, 'Was Aaron's death the reason you chose medicine?'

'Absolutely. I never wanted to be on the sidelines and feel that helpless again.'

'I totally get that.' She dropped his hand and reflexively rubbed her belly, like she often did. 'And your mum and dad? I can't imagine how they coped losing a child.'

'You wouldn't wish that pain on anyone.' He moved his gaze away from her belly, not wanting to think about the baby. A child who'd need guidance, wisdom and a great deal of looking after—things he wasn't able to offer. 'They kept busy. Way too busy. They organised a rural road safely campaign in Aaron's memory and Mum decided to start the guesthouse so she could care for everyone because she couldn't care for Aaron. Jenny and Ken were amazing with their perfect blend of no-nonsense support.

'Not everyone in town knew what to say or do and they either ignored us or smothered us or, worse still, laid their grief on us. That's hard to cope with. The town knew I was

there when it happened and having someone tell you that you
"*must really miss your brother*" when every moment of your
day is a reminder that he's not here because of something
you did almost sent me off the rails. If I hadn't had the goal
of medicine to honour Aaron, I think I would have dropped
out of school and left Jindi.'

Her face filled with empathy. 'And that's why you've never
told me this story?'

He nodded, thankful she understood. 'Once I arrived at
uni, I never mentioned Aaron or told anyone about him. I
needed space from the way people looked at me with a combination of pity and censure. That's what I meant when I said
small towns with their intimacy in your life can be stifling.'

She chewed her thumbnail, deep in thought. 'Is that how
it is with us now?'

'What?' He had no clue what she was asking him.

'Stifling. Knowing too much about each other.'

'Hell, no.' He reached out, grabbing her hand as the past
receded and the all-important present begged for attention.
'It's never been like that. Why would you even think that?'

Her large coffee-brown eyes filled with consternation. 'I
have no clue what's going on with us. That kiss under the
mistletoe—'

'Sorry,' he blurted out guiltily.

'No.' She shook her head. 'Don't be sorry. You know as
well as I do that if Rupert hadn't arrived when he did, he
may well have found your mouth and my hands considerably lower.'

He grinned at her, remembering the heat that had sizzled
between them. 'Yeah.'

Her olive skin didn't blush but her cheeks glowed, and unlike in the past when she would have dropped her gaze and
avoided a tricky topic, she now kept her eyes fixed on his.
'What I don't understand is why you did it. You've hardly

been able to look me in the eye since you got back from India and we both know that I've never been your type.'

He heard unexpected pain in her voice and he scanned her face, hating it that he'd inadvertently hurt her. He attempted to justify and explain but all he could come up with was, 'You're my friend, Georgie.'

Her mouth tweaked up one side. 'Exactly, and because of that we've *never* stuck our tongues down each other's throats.'

He stroked a damp strand of chestnut hair behind her ear. 'We got close once, though, remember?'

She nodded briskly and crossed her arms as if she was fighting to stay separate from him. 'And we decided it was a *bad* idea. Surely it still is? What I don't get is why now? I'm pregnant and so far removed from slim and sexy it's ridiculous.'

'No.' The word shot out hard and fast, riding on a wave of lust and chased by a need to reassure her. 'It's not ridiculous at all.'

Her eyes widened to huge black discs, making her look more gorgeous than ever, and his heart rate picked up, pushing hot and needy blood through him. Every part of him wanted to hold her and kiss her. Hell, who was he kidding? He wanted so much more than just holding and kissing.

Georgie heard his words raining over her and she wanted to hold on to them for ever, but she lived in the real world, even if the past week had been far from real. 'I think your nine months of no sex has caught up with you and it's got you acting crazy.'

He gripped his temples with his thumb and ring finger, and his expression was both painful and imploring. 'Come on, Georgie, be honest. You can't pin all of this on me. You kissed me like I was the last man standing.'

I know I did. She rolled her shoulders against the memory. 'At least I can blame pregnancy hormones. What's your excuse?'

'You.' The word stroked like a caress.

'Me?' Her voice squeaked in disbelief.

His eyes darkened to midnight-blue. 'Yes, you. You radiate an intoxicating power of femininity that cuts me off at the knees every time I see you.'

Her mouth fell open in stunned surprise. *I'm sexy? He wants me?* Her brain struggled to comprehend but her body automatically responded to the compliment, swaying slightly as her hips tilted and her breasts rose.

Despite having been in two long-term relationships, she'd never been aware of having any sexual power in her life. Everything inside her wanted to step straight into his arms and float away on a sea of pleasure, but she fought for common sense—for the much-needed protection for herself and her baby.

'How can I be all that when I'm pregnant?'

'Believe me—' his voice rasped out '—you're glorious.'

'I have sagging breasts and stretch marks.'

He stepped in close, his citrus scent circling her, and he rested his hands lightly on the sash of her robe. 'Let me be the judge.'

A hot and seductive tingle swooped through her until it settled as an insistent throb between her legs. It took every ounce of her energy to maintain the slight gap between them and not fall against his chest. 'Hamish, as much as I love being told I'm glorious, you told me three days ago that you don't find pregnant women sexy.'

'I don't.' Regret, confusion and guilt swam across his face. 'God, sorry, no, I mean I didn't.' He rolled his hands out in bewilderment. 'Until you.'

A shielding streak a mile wide spread through her. 'Has this got anything to do with you and *my* baby?'

He shook his head. 'Yes. No. Not the way you mean.' He

blew out a breath. 'You pregnant…you're stunningly sexy and I want you. God, I've wanted you from the moment I saw you in my house. But that's separate from the baby. It's *your* baby, Georgie, and, like we discussed, neither of us want me involved.'

That was one question answered—two, actually—but she still didn't totally understand. 'So why did you lie to me?'

His jaw tightened as if he was in pain. 'Because we're friends and our friendship means everything to me and I don't want to lose it or you. We both agreed all those years ago that neither of us wanted to take the risk that sex might change everything. Because you're about to start the sort of life I don't want and I didn't want to muddy things between us, and because we're staying at Weeroona with my family—'

'But we're not now,' she said quietly, as the realisation wove through her that he'd been struggling with *exactly* the same feelings that had been tormenting her.

'No, not tonight.' His eyes seemed to be sucking her into their sea-blue depths like a rip tide.

She swallowed. 'So…?'

'So…?'

The low rumble of his voice was like a long, delicious stroke of his hand and she shivered. 'We could just ignore the attraction like we've been doing.'

One of his hands toyed with the end of the sash while the other outlined the curve of her ear. 'We could do that, although has it really been working for us?'

A river of warm, liquid pleasure rode up and down her spine, threatening all rational thought, and she struggled to find her voice. 'We're adults. We're supposed to make wise and sensible choices.'

'You make wise and sensible decisions. I'm not known for that so much.'

'But making out will complicate things even further.' She appealed to his common sense, needing it now because she was so close to giving in to the attraction—consequences be damned. 'Like you said, won't it change everything between us?'

The twinkle in his eye, which was as much a part of him as his blond hair, faded. It was replaced by a serious look while his fingers continued to rub her ear gently. 'It's already changed. You know it has and perhaps this would act like a reset button.'

Her head tilted into his hand as if worried she might miss a moment of his delicious touch. 'Sex as a reset button?' Not even saying it out loud was enough to jolt her away from the idea.

'Why not? Ignoring it isn't working. It's just driving us both around the twist.' His ragged voice struck a chord that echoed deep inside her. 'Join me in not overthinking this.'

He had a point. A very delicious point. Nothing she'd tried had made any impact on dampening her need for him and she wanted their easy camaraderie back. They weren't two people who'd just met. She knew and trusted him and she'd be lying to herself if she said in all the years they'd been friends she'd never wondered what sex would be like with him. This wasn't a pledge of a future together. Neither of them wanted that because their future needs and wants were so very different. No, this was pure lust needing to be sated. To be got out of the way so they could get their friendship back.

Heady with her newly discovered sexual power, she gave him what she hoped was a sultry look. 'You find me unbelievably sexy now that I'm pregnant?'

'God, yes.'

At that moment she wanted to kiss him so badly it hurt, but she still had something else she needed to say. 'Based on that logic, once I've had the baby and go back to my pre-pregnant size and shape, you'll no longer feel that way. Promise me things will be back to the way they were? Good friends?'

They had to. She was never risking being left by a man again. Not risking her heart or her baby's.

'Like I said, it will act as a reset.'

His breath brushed her cheek and desire almost toppled the doubt that had sneaked in. 'Haim, I haven't had sex since before—'

He put his finger to her lips. 'Shh, stop analysing this. There's more than one way to have sex. Let's just see where it goes and enjoy exploring each other's bodies.'

Her head fell back as she recalled the words he'd said to her in their first conversation way back at university. 'Live a little. I guess we don't have to worry about condoms.'

His eyes twinkled with wicked intent. 'Exactly, and that on its own is an incredible turn-on. George…' His fingers softly pressed her chin downwards so she was looking him straight in the eye. 'No matter what happens, I promise you, it will be fun.'

His caring reassurance blew away the last threads of her restraint. 'I plan to hold you to that.' She tugged at the hem of his top, quickly pulling it over his head and ignoring his shout of surprise. She pressed her palms against his hot, golden skin. 'You have the most gorgeous chest.'

'I think I'm supposed to say that to you.' His voice was hoarse as she trailed her fingers across the indentations on his tight abdomen.

She laughed, intoxicated on being desired, and with an unfamiliar flare of sexual courage she lifted her chin and slowly undid the sash of her dressing gown.

Hamish watched stunned and mesmerised at the woman in front of him. He knew her and yet he didn't know her at all. Proud and mind-blowingly sexy, Georgie opened the edges of her gown, seductively sliding them over burnished and glowing skin, over full and heavy breasts with their areolas large and dark and nipples ripe and ready, until finally letting it fall fully open, exposing a taut, round baby belly that was beyond beautiful.

A lump rose in his throat for the briefest of moments before heat roared through him, obliterating everything except raw and primal lust. Looking was no longer enough. He wanted to bury his face in her breasts, feel the weight of them in his hands and the touch of them in his mouth. He wanted the feel of her hair running through his fingers, to cup her curves with his palms and...*he just wanted all of her.*

'You're beautiful and I'm blessed.' He reached out his hands, linked fingers with hers and pulled her into him before dipping his head.

Her lips opened to meet his, capturing them, and his plan of plundering and raiding her mouth stalled under her tempting assault. This sexually dominant Georgie was an unexpected and delicious aphrodisiac, and he'd never been so aroused in his life.

As her tongue worked its magic, her hands roamed over his shoulders, down his spine and lingered in the dip on his lower back. Silver spots rained over him as he pulled in increasingly shallow breaths and every part of him throbbed with pleasurable pain.

Then her lips were on his chest, her tongue trailing a warm, damp path slowly downwards until she sucked his nipple into her mouth, and white heat speared through him, threatening his barely held control.

His hands moved, cupping the sides of her head, tilting it back from him so he was losing himself in the velvet depths of her wide and lust-filled eyes. Somehow he managed to grind out the word, 'Bed.'

Taking her hand, and with a restraint that astounded him, he walked her slowly to one of the two double beds, pulled back the soft white comforter and lowered her. Again he stared at her beautiful body, which seemed to be lit from the inside out.

In a matching glance her eyes drifted down his body, lingering on his erection, which was barely disguised by the pants of his scrubs. 'It doesn't seem quite fair that you're still half-dressed.'

'You distracted me.'

She smiled and lifted her hands behind her head, her breasts rising with the action. 'Did I?'

With a groan, he shucked his pants and knelt on the bed. 'I had no idea you were so good at this.'

She rolled towards him with a self-conscious laugh. 'Neither did I. Am I really?'

'Believe me, Georgie, you're a fantasy come true.'

He kissed her, only this time he took control, loving the soft groans that came from her. Groans of need that he'd created. And then his face was finally pillowed in her soft, amazing breasts, and his mouth closed over a dark and erotic nipple. He was home.

Georgie cried out, a sob catching in her throat.

His head shot up so fast a pain burned his neck, and he suddenly remembered a note about tender breasts from a university lecture on pregnancy. 'God, sorry, did I hurt you?'

Her fingers gripped his head, frantically pushing it back down. 'No, it was…it's… Just keep doing it.'

Relief blew through him. 'My pleasure.' He centred all his attention on her breasts, his tongue flicking and his teeth lightly scraping. She writhed and panted with pleasure and his blood pounded with an excitement he'd not felt in… He'd *never* felt anything like this. He'd never had a woman respond to him in this way and he couldn't get enough of it. He moved his body, straddling her legs.

Lying on her side, she stared at him through glassy eyes. 'Do you want to—?'

'No hurry.' Somehow, he managed to say those words despite his body telling him otherwise. He gazed at her belly as if he was looking at it for the first time, and in a way he was. Her belly button had flattened and blue veins ran just under the tight and shiny skin.

He reached out his hand, hovering it just above the bump, and then she breathed out and it rose against his hand. Smooth skin tightened under his touch—a tiny ripple of movement as if to say, *I'm here too*.

His chest tightened.

He'd taught himself to think of Georgie as pregnant—a state of being rather than the precursor to the arrival of an actual child—but touching her like this exposed the lie he'd told himself. His child grew there.

No. Georgie's baby.

He severed the contact, moving both his hands to the lower part her thighs. She lifted her top leg, resting it on his shoulder, and he traced ever-decreasing circles until they pressed gently into the sensitive skin high on her inner thigh. Then he carefully lowered his head and his mouth met her damp and ready flesh.

Georgie's hips bucked of their own accord when Hamish's tongue found her clitoris. If she'd thought the exquisite pain he'd taunted her with when he'd suckled her breasts couldn't be bettered, then she'd been seriously deluded. With each stroke of his tongue the tingling shafts of pleasure built on the previous one and she was barely aware of his hands gently holding her hips still so he could maintain his delicious contact.

Her head thrashed against the pillow as her hands gripped the mattress and she hardly recognised her voice when she heard herself say, 'Oh, God, Hamish, just there, yes.'

Then the power of speech failed her as the spiralling towers of pleasure toppled, spreading waves of wonder through every part of her. As her ragged breathing slowed, her twitching muscles made her feel empty and she rolled onto her back and stretched out her hands.

Hamish pulled her to sitting position and she immediately knelt so they were chest to chest. 'Thank you. That was amazing.'

His eyes burned with need for her as she ran her hands down his chest lightly, skimming lower across his stomach until her hand stroked the hot, hard shaft of his penis.

He shivered and kissed her. 'It won't take much, Georgie. Watching you come nearly undid me.'

She smiled at the thrill his words gave her and she held them close. It still amazed her that he found her so erotic when she'd thought pregnancy had rendered her undesirable, but she loved the feeling all the same. Her fingers stalled on their errand. 'We can't risk that, then.'

He glanced down at her hand. 'I thought that was the point.'

She kissed him swiftly, her tongue dancing in his mouth so she could taste all of him. 'I want you inside me when you come. I want to feel you.'

His brows drew down as his gaze skimmed her belly for a moment before rising again to her face. 'Are you sure?'

She nodded, feeling blood rushing to her cheeks making them burn, which was ridiculous seeing as she was naked and had just had an orgasm in front of him. 'I've done some reading.'

This time one brow rose and a bone-melting grin split his face.

She laughed and told the truth. 'Okay, I did an internet search on my phone after you kissed me. Late-pregnancy sex calls for some inventiveness and I'm guessing you're up for that.'

'Just tell me where you want me.'

Even joking, his deep voice sent her blood scudding to every pulse point and her breathing hitched up. 'There are a few options...' She pushed him gently onto his back and gave him another long kiss, soaking him into her skin, her muscle and every cell before she pulled away.

His eyes gleamed. 'I'm liking it so far.'

She laughed again and the contrast hit her. She'd never been this relaxed during first-time sex with anyone. Not that she had vast experience but she'd had enough to know that the first time was usually fraught with *Should I do this? Should I say that?* because the relationship was in its infancy. Sex with Hamish was devoid of all that, plus she had a confidence she'd never experienced before.

She kissed him again. 'The thing about all fours is that I can't kiss you.'

'But I can kiss you.'

'True, but I miss out.' She glanced at the chair by the bed and let go of her final reticence. 'We move to that chair and you sit in it and I straddle you. That is if you think you can hold me.'

'You're hardly huge, Georgie. Let's try it.' He threw a towel over the chair, sat down and held out his arms.

She moved into them and slowly lowered herself down on him, feeling herself opening in delicious increments to fully take him. She sighed.

He tensed. 'Is it comfortable?'

'It feels divine.' Resting her arms on the side of the chair she leaned in and kissed him. 'You can move too, you know.'

'Like this?' He sounded uncertain.

She moved with him. 'Exactly like this.'

With his eyes fixed on hers, he filled her, stroking her sweetly with long, gentle thrusts.

'Oh, yes. Right there,' she managed to pant out as the most intense waves of feeling she'd ever known built in her. 'Keep doing that…if it's working for you.'

His breathing was fast and ragged. 'Oh…it's working.'

And then their bodies found their rhythm and slowly the shape of the room slipped away, the feel of the chair vanished and the only thing that existed were his hands on her hips and the feel of him inside her, stroking her higher and higher until she was flung out beyond herself, taking him with her to a place neither of them had gone before.

CHAPTER TEN

SWEAT trickled into Hamish's eyes as he sank back in the chair, gasping for breath and waiting for his body to reassemble itself. He wasn't new to sex or to the momentous sensations that came with release but this, what had just happened between him and Georgie, felt like he'd been blown apart.

Georgie's head had fallen onto his shoulder and her legs twitched around him. He stroked her hair. 'You okay?'

She raised her head, her eyes soft and satisfied. 'Very okay. You?'

He twirled some of her hair through his fingers. 'Same.' The remnants of the orgasm were now slowly being replaced by liquid relaxation, which he knew would quickly bring sleep. 'You taught me something new tonight.'

Georgie kissed him on the forehead. 'I taught me something new as well. I might have to write a paper on it so all pregnant women can discover it.' She laughed as she shifted slightly and rose up. 'I need to lie down.'

He was instantly alert. 'Is everything all right?' He still couldn't quite bring himself to say, *'with the baby'.*

She gave him a knowing smile. *'Everything* is fine but I'm thirty-five and my hips are going to explode if I sit in this position much longer. Bed is totally inviting.'

She fell back onto the mattress and immediately rolled onto her side. He slid in next to her and it seemed the most

natural thing in the world to cuddle up to her so that their
bodies rested against each other like spoons in a drawer. He
slipped his leg between hers and rested his top arm across
her hip, his fingers adapting to the lower curve of her belly.

Her hair tickled his face. 'It makes sense for us to drive
back to Weeroona in your car in the morning.'

He waited for her to reply, but she didn't say a word.
'George?'

She cleared her throat. 'I've arranged for a prenatal appointment at eleven.'

He hated how she sounded uncomfortable telling him that,
but he knew the reason lay wholly and solely at his own feet.
Still, he couldn't quite get past it. 'No problem. We'll leave
after that.'

Her fingers fiddled with the top sheet. 'Or you could go
back to Weeroona and I could stay here one more night if
they have room. Then, when your floors are finished, stay
at your place.'

Her plan, which six days ago would have been perfect,
now seemed plain wrong. 'And miss the famous Pettigrew
fancy-dress Christmas party that wraps up the reunion in a
couple of days? It's always fun, plus the family would make
my life hell if you didn't come.'

'Well…' Her voice was so soft and full of hesitation that
he had to strain to hear. 'I guess, as your best friend, protecting you from your family *is* part of my job.'

'Damn straight.' He kissed her neck and his arm tightened
around her for a moment in a reassuring gesture. Georgie's
belly tightened under his arm and he felt a sudden thump
against his hand. His entire body went rigid. Another thump
followed, jolting his palm—the baby was kicking against
him.

Touching him.

Making contact with him.

He waited for the expected waves of horror to spin him

round and round, making him want to run and run fast the way they usually did whenever he thought about Georgie's baby, but it didn't happen. Instead, awe and wonder streamed through him, forming gossamer strands of connection that wrapped around his heart.

His DNA.

His baby.

His.

He pressed his lips to her bare shoulder, suddenly feeling ridiculously proud that he'd helped make a baby. 'I think he liked what we were just doing.'

A spurt of laughter made her body twitch from head to toe. 'I hate to impinge on your manhood, but Widget always gets active at this time of night. It's ironic, really, given it's the time I fall into bed, craving sleep.' She suddenly sat up, pulling the sheet with her.

Cool air rushed in where she'd been nestled against him and he rested his hand on the middle of her back. 'Do you need something?'

She gazed down at him. 'Food. I'm absolutely starving.'

A burr of guilt prickled him and he shot her a grin. 'I guess we got a bit distracted and forgot to eat.' He reached over to the bedside table and picked up the room-service menu. 'But that's easy fixed. What do you—?'

'A hamburger with the lot, including beetroot and pineapple, a large caramel milkshake and a banana.'

He laughed. 'Are you sure? I mean, you don't sound at all certain about the order.'

She gave him a playful thump and scrambled over him, trying to reach the phone. 'Never tease a pregnant woman about food, especially when she hasn't eaten in way too long and is hungry for anything.'

Her hair fell forward like liquid chocolate, brushing his chest with tantalising flicks. He licked his lips, wanting to kiss her again. 'I'm hungry for you.'

Her lips curved up in a secret but sexy smile and she low-ered her head and whispered, 'Feed me and I'm yours.'

In his haste to get to the phone he knocked it flying and when he finally retrieved it, he ordered the food and paid the premium for fast service.

Georgie put her hand on the car-door handle as Hamish slowed down close to the maternity section of the hospital. It felt a bit odd having Hamish at the wheel of her car and she'd had to let go of her natural response of insisting that she be the one to drive. Eventually, she'd conceded to her-self that it made sense for him to drive because he could run errands, including picking up some things for the costume party, while she kept her appointment. 'Drop me here if it's easier and I'll text you when I've finished.'

Hamish ignored her and turned left into the staff car park. 'I thought I'd come with you.'

She stared at him as her brain scrabbled to work out where this totally unexpected comment had come from. They'd spent a wonderful night together and while she'd been snug-gled up to him with his arm looped loosely around her, she'd slept more soundly than she had in a long time.

Her body still tingled from the gentle and delicious way he'd woken her, giving a whole new meaning to the word *spooning*.

All the superlatives in the world couldn't even begin to describe how amazing the sex between them had been. Even so, she was really proud of herself because only for the brief-est of moments had she allowed herself to spin castles in the air and daydream about Hamish, herself and the baby being a family. Thankfully, she'd metaphorically smacked herself around the head with a wet noodle very quickly and had re-minded herself of Jonas and Luke.

They'd left her. They hadn't loved her enough to want to give her a family and a future, and she was never going to let anyone hurt her like that again. It was the reason she was doing motherhood alone. Besides, Hamish's track record with relationships was short, sharp and never longer than six months, and she wanted a lifetime. They loved each other as *friends* and that had to be enough.

She refused to examine the circle of sadness that ringed her heart whenever she thought about it. She wanted so badly for Hamish to see that he'd been too young to be responsible for his brother's actions and to let that pain go, but she could see how strongly it influenced him. Something that significant didn't change overnight. He couldn't envisage himself as a father and she had to accept that.

Yes, last night had been the best sex of her life, but there was no way she was letting it trick her into thinking it meant more. It had only been sex and as Hamish had said, a *reset button* for their friendship. A reset button that had worked.

He'd been relaxed all morning, making jokes and being the Hamish she knew so well. The sexual tension that had boiled so strongly between them had definitely been sated and was now a low simmer in the background. Most importantly, their friendship was front and centre again, as it should be, and their easy camaraderie was finally back.

There'd been no uncomfortable 'morning after sex' stuff either. In fact, she'd been pleasantly surprised when he'd actually remembered that her favourite breakfast was bircher muesli and had ordered it up for her and had had it waiting for her after her shower. She'd been even more stunned that he'd thought to give her one of his old T-shirts and a pair of baggy pants she could wear instead of the scrubs, and avoid confusing the staff at the hospital. Hamish had always been fun but not always quite so attentive.

Which led her back to him mentioning the appointment. 'Come with me?' She wasn't quite able to stop the rising inflection of her voice. 'To the clinic?'

He parked and killed the engine before pulling the keys

from the ignition and giving her a familiar smile. 'Unless you have a problem with it?'

Yes. No. I don't know. 'I… Really? You want to come?'

He shrugged. 'I thought it might be a good idea just in case.'

The words sent up a flag. 'Just in case what?'

'You go into labour down at Jindi. I haven't delivered a baby in a year or so.'

Before she could reply, he got out of the car and came around to her side and opened the door.

She rose from her seat and rested her hand on the door as a slew of defensive emotions battered her. Hamish didn't belong in the labour-ward picture. He didn't belong in any pictures of her and the baby. 'And you won't need to deliver this one.'

He folded his arms across his chest she'd so thoroughly explored last night. 'Exactly how many weeks are you?'

She blinked. He'd never wanted to know anything about the baby and she'd been deliberately vague about it to all the Pettigrews except Denise. 'Not enough for you to be worrying about it being born in Jindi in an ER-style delivery.'

He shrugged and gave a mild smile. 'I'm not worried but, unlike you, I do know where the clinic is located so I'll walk you there and it will save you getting lost.'

She couldn't argue with that and as long as he wasn't coming into the examination room with her, she was fine with him walking her there. She'd never worked at Geelong Hospital so was unfamiliar with the layout. Her doctor in Melbourne had organised the appointment for her and when she'd asked his receptionist, 'Where do I go?', her reply had been, 'Read the signs.'

As they walked into the clinic, one of the midwives greeted Hamish with a familiar touch to his arm and a wide and flirty smile. 'Dr Pettigrew, what brings you to Maternity?'

While Hamish was introducing her to the midwife as his

'good friend and colleague', Georgie swallowed, realising she too was now part of a fair-sized club of women who'd slept with Hamish. Women he'd loved and left.

An unexpected shot of jealousy caught her in her solar plexus, and she caught her breath on a rip of air that made her cough.

But you don't want a relationship with him. You were saving a friendship. That's totally different from all those other women.

Hamish's hand settled lightly on her lower back. 'Would you like me to get you some water?'

She nodded, mostly so she could pull herself together before his keen gaze saw more than she wanted him to. Before he'd returned, the doctor called her name and suddenly she was in the examination room. That bit of good timing had just solved the problem of Hamish.

A moment later he slipped in, holding a glass of water, and Susan Meir, the obstetrician, glanced up from the sheaf of fax papers that were Georgie's medical notes from her doctor in Melbourne. She gave him a friendly nod.

'Perfect timing as usual, Hamish. By the way, can you thank your mother for the gingerbread-house kit? The girls have had a lovely time making it.'

'Get them to text her a photo. She'd be thrilled to see their creation.' Smiling, Hamish dropped easily into the chair next to Georgie.

She did a double-take. She hadn't expected him to follow her into the room, let alone stay, but unless she was prepared to have a scene in front of one of his colleagues and a family friend, and set the gossip mill in motion—and neither of them could afford that—it seemed Hamish was attending the appointment. Unease eddied through her.

While Susan measured her belly, took her blood pressure and did all the usual routine checks, Hamish sat on the other side of the screen. The only time she heard him make a sound—and it was a strangled sort of a noise—was when the sonogram blared out the galloping beat of the baby's heart rate. When Georgie was dressed again and reseated on the other side of the desk, Susan put down her pen and leaned forward.

'Your blood pressure is fantastic, there's no sign of any protein in your urine and you're probably making every other pregnant woman jealous by the fact your ankles are not remotely swollen.'

'Pregnancy suits her,' Hamish said, giving Georgie a wink.

Was he mad? Was he trying to give everything away to a family friend? She tried to send him a *shut-up* message by tilting her head and widening her eyes at him but he'd glanced away.

Susan continued, 'The baby's heart rate is fine too, but the baby hasn't grown since your last visit to your doctor. I'm not overly concerned but, that said, we need to keep an eye on things. Have you been eating enough, getting enough rest?'

Georgie bit her lip. 'The last week has been—'

'I'll make sure she gets the rest she needs.' Hamish's hand patted Georgie's shoulder as if she were a child. 'And Denise will feed her up so the baby won't be able to do anything but grow.'

Susan's faint worry lines faded and were replaced with a smile. 'That sounds perfect.'

Georgie raised her shoulder, shrugging off his hand. 'Your mother's busy enough with—'

'I know from experience that it's best just to let the Pettigrews take care of you,' Susan said with a laugh. 'The summer I was pregnant with my third, Denise insisted we holiday at Weeroona. She kept Jeremy and the girls so busy that I hardly saw them and all I was allowed to do was laze by the pool and read. It's almost worth getting pregnant again just for the *me* time.

'But seriously, Georgina, please rest, and enjoy Denise's healthy food. You and your baby are in the best of hands.'

And then Susan was on her feet, which was code for *The appointment is over*, goodbyes were being said and Hamish was opening the door and ushering her out into the corridor.

'I'll get the car and meet you downstairs,' Hamish called over his shoulder as his long strides took him quickly away from her.

Georgie was left standing with her mouth opening and closing as a rush of words—*I can walk across the street* and *I'm not mentally incapable of making my own decisions about what's best for my baby*—tried to get air time, only they came out as a guttural 'Uh!'

Hamish didn't pause in his stride or even look back, and she was left feeling like she was a bystander in her own life.

Georgie slowly opened her eyes, blinking against dappled light that came through the trees. She must have dozed off on the pool lounger that Denise and Hamish had relocated under a tree and insisted that she rest on while the rest of the Pettigrews were off on a rogaining excursion. She wondered why they didn't just call the reunion the Pettigrew Olympics and be done with it.

As her eyes came into focus, she realised Hamish was squatting down next to her, his hand lightly resting on her thigh and a smile on his face. He smelled of sweat, energy and something that was quintessentially Hamish. He glanced around quickly before leaning in and briefly sweeping his lips across hers. 'Good nap?'

'It was.' She stretched out with a smile, totally relaxed, and then she touched his cheek. 'I don't usually nap but a certain someone kept me up late last night.'

She expected his eyes to darken in the shared memory of great sex—the best sex she'd ever known—but instead his expression shot to serious and a tiny part of her shrivelled.

He nodded slowly. 'That's what I want to talk about.'

All her relaxation disappeared. *He's going to remind you the sex was a one-off deal.*

She bit her lip. She was a sensible adult and they had an agreement that she believed in totally. Even so, she pressed back against the lounge, trying hard not to let the odd feeling inside her gain any more weight. They were back at Weeroona and nothing could happen.

The weight inside her started to chafe and her chin lifted. 'I'm your *friend*, Hamish. Please spare me the post-sex speech you use on your young twenty-somethings when you've had enough of them.'

He flinched and for a crazy moment she thought she saw hurt in his eyes.

He removed his hand from her thigh. 'I *was* going to say as much as I loved the time we spent in Geelong, you need to take things easy for your and the baby's health, and because of what Susan said, that probably means no sex.'

She instantly felt small for having misread him, and yet the chafing increased at the way he was suddenly fussing over her. 'I'm the one who makes those sorts of decisions.'

His brows drew down and he studied her. 'Spit it out, George. What's bothering you?'

His straight-up gaze speared her. This was a perfect example of the best and worst thing about being such close friends—he knew her too well. Still, he'd just given her a chance to clear the air. 'You're taking over, Hamish.' *And I can't let you do that or I won't survive.*

'How?'

'Cutting me off in mid-sentence with Susan Meir, telling her you had it all under control, as if I don't have a say.'

He looked utterly flummoxed. 'I'm only trying to help.'

And she knew he was but she'd been looking after herself and the baby for eight months, and she was going to be looking after the baby alone for the next twenty years so she couldn't allow herself to get used to this sort of pampering when she knew it wasn't going to last. She rested her hand on his arm. 'Thank you, but can you help by waiting to be asked?'

His mouth and nose seemed to move a full circle around his face as if he was battling with his answer, and then he gave her a wry smile. 'I can promise to try.'

'I can't ask for much more than that.'

His hand brushed her belly lightly. 'Hey, Widget, your mother's really stubborn.'

Surprise tumbled through her. Up until today Hamish had been so strung out about the baby that he'd never talked to him before. She knew his gift of life had come with a lot of reservations on his part, all of which had played out over this past week, so she was pleased he'd relaxed enough to be able to include the baby in the teasing. He was great with kids, although by their mutual decision he wouldn't be having much to do with this one.

Never say never.

Self-protection had her immediately squashing the thought.

The Pettigrew family reunion Christmas party was the final event of the week-long gathering, and it was in full swing. Weeroona glowed with the twinkle of white fairy-lights strung across the veranda and draped in the trees, casting a magical spell, despite the fact the sun hadn't quite set and the air was warm. Children charged around everywhere, excited about their costumes and checking out everyone else's, while the band—a ragtag ensemble of Pettigrews playing the fiddle, banjo, mouth organ, piano accordion, bush bass, lagerphone, guitar and saw—were tuning up for the bush dance.

'Uncle Hamish!' Rupert bounded up, wrapping his arms around Hamish's knees.

Ever since Hamish had let him turn on the Christmas-tree lights, Rupe had been seeking him out and he'd enjoyed having the little guy around. Laughing, he put his hands on his nephew's furry head and pointy ears. 'Exactly how are kangaroos part of Christmas?'

Rupert put his 'paws' on his hips and gave Hamish a look that questioned his adoration. 'I'm a white boomer. I pull Santa's sleigh.' He hopped off, presumably looking for the rest of the mob of kangaroos.

'You need to brush up on your Christmas traditions, bro,' Ben said, chuckling. He was wearing what looked like a Weeroona tea-towel on his head, white baggy pants and an old dressing gown with a silk rope tie. He flicked Hamish's red T-shirt a disappointing glance. 'Shame you didn't have time to at least raid Mum's tea-towel cupboard. Now we've only got two wise men for the costume parade.'

Hamish accepted the proffered beer from Ben and twisted the top off. 'Not to worry, big brother. You and Caleb are wise enough for the three of us. Cheers.' He clinked the long neck of his bottle against his brother's.

Ben frowned. 'Hamish—'

'How's Ken?' Caleb joined them, wearing a real *kaffiyeh* instead of a tea-towel.

Hamish had been getting updates from the hospital twice a day for the past two days. 'He's stabilising. If he keeps on like this he'll be moved out of ICU into the high-dependency unit. He's got months of rehab ahead of him, but he's up for that.'

Ben nodded. 'He's a tough old bugger but, hell, I haven't been able to get the picture of him under that limb out of my head.'

Hamish studied his older brother. He couldn't ever re-member seeing him rattled. Usually Ben was teasing him or giving him instructions or suggesting he get his personal life organised, but right now Ben was looking decidedly un-sure about himself. 'It's called "bystander trauma" and it's real. I want you to focus on the fact you were a vital part of the rescue team.'

'I didn't do much,' Ben said.

Hamish shook his head. 'Without Caleb and Dad, and your skill with a chainsaw, we'd have lost valuable time and we might have lost Ken. You did good.' He squeezed Ben's shoulder, remembering how great it had felt debriefing with Georgie about the emergency.

'I'm happy to listen or answer any questions you have about any of it. It's my experience that talking about it helps shift it out of your head.'

Undisguised admiration crossed Ben's face. 'I don't know how you do it, Hamish. Day in day out, working like that without totally losing it. Thank God you do, though. If I was ever in a position like Ken, I'd want you on my team.'

'Hell, yeah!' Caleb joined Ben in raising his bottle of beer to him in a toast and slapping him on the back. 'The world needs talented doctors like you.'

'Thanks.' The word came out on a croak, and he found he couldn't say more. The unexpected compliments had moisture misting behind his eyes and he took a long draft of his beer to mask the surge of emotion.

Get a grip. Reacting like this was crazy, and he sure as hell wasn't going to bawl like a girl just because, for the first time he could ever remember, his brothers had finally acknowledged him as more than their irresponsible little brother. He turned to give himself some extra recovery seconds and to try and think of something smart and offhand to say, and his gaze collided with his two sisters-in-law and Georgie. They were stepping out of the house and onto the lawn.

Beer spurted out of his nose as Ben gasped and Caleb gave a long, low whistle.

Ben high-fived Caleb. 'Bro, we married them and each of us is going to get lucky tonight.'

'Happy holidays,' Caleb said with a grin a mile wide.

But it wasn't Annie and Erin's male fantasy of 'Santa's little helpers', wearing red with white fur-trim bustiers, that had Hamish hot and hard. It was Georgie. How the hell had she managed to take a classic Christmas tradition like a plum pudding and make it sexy?

She had, though, and how. Her tanned and shapely legs were bare from the tips of her toes to the tops of her toned thighs and only then, at bikini-line level, did fabric touch her. Her baby bump and breasts were wrapped in unbleached calico, giving her the roundness of a plum pudding. The calico was cut away under her arms, leaving her shoulders deliciously bare, before tying at her throat and fanning out like the top of a pudding cloth. Her hair was swept up on top of her head and she wore a wreath of holly.

He couldn't tear his eyes off her.

'Georgie's not too shabby either,' Ben added.

'You're married and she's pregnant,' Hamish ground out, as a visceral need to protect her swamped him.

Ben raised one brow. 'I remember when Annie was pregnant with Jack.' He sounded almost wistful. 'God, the sex was good then. Not that it isn't now, but it was different. Like her body craved it more.'

'There's something almost primal about knowing you helped make that baby,' Caleb agreed. 'Plus not having to worry about contraception is an added, uninhibited bonus.'

Hamish choked as his brothers described exactly his own experience with Georgie.

'You all right there, Hamish?' Ben asked with a grin.

'Shut up.' Hamish wished he could be anywhere else but walking away at this moment would be difficult.

'You know what I think?' Ben said, fixing his gaze firmly on Hamish.

He tried to deflect. 'Even if I said I did, you'd still tell me anyway, right?'

Ben glanced at Caleb and then back again. 'I think Hamish has got it bad for his pregnant friend.'

Panic boiled inside him. 'Don't be ridiculous.'

'Oh, I'm not.' The teasing faded from Ben's eyes. 'Georgina's a hell of a woman, Hamish, and she runs rings around the types you've been dating since you were seventeen. I don't understand why you didn't snap her up years ago.'

'And here we go again. Not every man has to have a wife, three kids and a people mover to be happy, Ben.' It was his standard response to hide the truth, one he used whenever his brothers brought up his lack of commitment, but today it sounded strangely hollow.

'That's true, but it's pretty awesome when you do.' Caleb's gaze drifted to Erin, who was now squatting and giving Rupert a hug. 'Mum said Georgie used donor sperm so there's no guy on the scene, right?'

She used my sperm. It's my baby. 'That's right, no guy.' Why the hell did his throat feel so tight?

'You'd be a fool, Hamish, if you let a nameless man's child stop you from telling her how you feel,' Ben said.

The usual frustrations his older brother always generated poured through him. '*Don't* tell me what I'm feeling, Ben. You have absolutely no clue.'

'Neither do you, and that's the problem. Do you think we're blind, mate? From the moment you and Georgie arrived here, you've been distracted. You're always looking at her and the last two days you've been clucking around her as if it was your kid she's incubating.'

Dread took huge chunks out of his self-control as his heart slammed against his chest. He tried to make his voice sound disinterested. 'I'm a doctor and she's pregnant. It goes with the territory.'

'It's more than that,' Caleb said, 'and you know it. You've spent heaps of time with the boys this year compared with any other. Erin reckons for the first time ever you're trying on fatherhood for size.'

He wanted to shout, *Erin knows squat*, but his sister-in-law was a lawyer and an emotionally intelligent woman who saw far too much for his peace of mind. Desperate, he grabbed onto adversarial tactics. 'Ben would disagree with her.'

'No, I wouldn't,' Ben said quickly, his tone slightly injured. 'Look, I don't understand why a brilliant doctor and a seemingly intelligent man wants to keep playing the role of the irresponsible young—'

'I'm not...'

You don't have to play the role of the Pettigrew son who never grew up. The sound of Georgie's voice clear and loud in his head sucked the words back down. He blew out an unsteady breath. God, she was right.

I think that's how you saw it through your grief and trauma and you've let it play out that way ever since. You're allowed to want a family.

He froze, recognising for the very first time the way he'd lived his life. He'd been stepping up to the plate at work for years, fighting to save lives, but at home he'd let fear hold him hostage. He didn't want to be that person any more.

Ben stared at him for a few seconds, nonplussed and with concern in his eyes. 'Hamish?'

He shook his head. 'Sorry. What?'

'All I'm saying is that you're ready. You're an amazing doctor and you'll make an excellent father.'

'I know you hate it when Ben thinks he's right, Hamish, but this time he is,' Caleb said. 'You're different. Something's changed in you.'

He stared at his brothers, dumbfounded, and yet their words echoed deep down inside him, giving truth to the yet unnamed feelings that had been stirring ever since he'd made love to Georgie. Ever since thoughts of the baby had thrilled him rather than freaking him out, and the overwhelming need to protect them both had been stronger than his fear of making a mistake. All in all, it had made it difficult to hide his feelings. Hell, who was he kidding? He hadn't been able to hide it his feelings at all, and Georgie had noticed.

He'd spent the past two days finding excuses to touch Georgie's belly in the hope of feeling some or any baby movement, and at the prenatal appointment he'd recorded the sonogram's sound of the baby's heartbeat on his phone. At night, when all he'd wanted to do was go and crawl into bed and snuggle up to Georgie, he'd found himself listening to it while thoughts of sharing it all with Georgie filled his head. Thoughts he'd tried to run from but which today he wanted to hold fast to.

The idea of fatherhood no longer paralysed him. Instead, it excited him and for the first time in a long, long time it made him feel hopeful. More than anything, he wanted to try, and knowing he would be doing it with his best friend, the woman he loved, made him grin like a Cheshire cat.

I love her.

The realisation slid in like a perfect sigh—as if his world had finally came into complete alignment. Of course he loved her. God, how had he been so blind not to have realised that before? He'd loved her for years without knowing or understanding that all those wonderful feelings he had for her, how special she made him feel, was love.

He loved her and he wanted to be a father to their baby more than anything else in the world.

'You're ready for the biggest step of all,' said Ben, slapping him on the back. 'You'll ace it.'

He gave the tea-towel on his brother's head a tug. 'I *never* thought I'd ever say this, Ben, but I totally agree with you.'

CHAPTER ELEVEN

GEORGIE threw her head back in delight as the band played the final chord of the dance and Hamish spun her round in a twirl. They were the last couple to 'strip the willow' and with close to seventy people taking part it had been a very long dance up and down the centre. She'd loved every minute of it, especially as standing up was her current preferred position.

All in all, it had been a wonderful day. Hamish had been his fun self and he hadn't hovered too much, although she didn't let herself think about how hard she knew he was finding her request not to fuss because it just confused her. Instead, she'd pushed it all aside and enjoyed a real girls' afternoon with Annie and Erin as they'd created their costumes together. There'd been lots of laughter along with shared baby tips, which Georgie had found both useful and a little bit scary.

She'd been pleased to have the company, which had taken her mind off the fact that Widget's foot seemed to be stuck under her ribs and no matter how much she tried to push it down or move it, it wouldn't budge. It made sitting uncomfortable and gave her some occasional mild back pain. For the first time in the pregnancy she was really aware of the baby making it hard to find a position that was comfortable. She tried not to think about how she had another three weeks of this, along with the fact that after talking with Annie and Erin she felt very under-prepared for a baby.

Hamish's arm stayed loosely around what had once been her waist as the band gave a collective bow. After Nathan, the caller, announced they were taking a short break, everyone clapped their thanks and the parents of young children started the slow process of trying to put overwrought and tired kids to bed.

She smiled, loving how the entire day and now the evening had combined to give her everything she adored about Christmas—tradition, fun and family.

Widget would love all of this when he's older.

She'd pretty much accepted the baby would be a boy and a picture slowly built in her mind of him running around excitedly with his cousins. *No!* She instantly barred the thought. None of this could belong to her and the baby because the Pettigrews were not her family. She was doing all this on her own.

The remaining adults and teenagers drifted away to the drinks table and the clusters of chairs, and Denise gave them a beckoning wave. Georgie started to change direction but Hamish merely waved back, before steering her towards the towering beech trees on the boundary of the garden.

She paused. 'Um, shouldn't we go and talk to your mother?'

'Plenty of time for that later,' he said with a grin as his hand continued to gently propel her forward.

The white light of the first stars had started piercing the dusky sky and the night air settled over her like a warm caress.

'Having fun?' Hamish's breath stroked her ear and the tingles of need she'd thought they'd exorcised by having sex flared again.

'Absolutely,' she squeaked, then cleared her throat. 'Lots of fun.'

'Good.' His hands massaged her shoulders and he pressed a kiss into her hair.

A skitter of unease dampened her need. 'Haim, it's not totally dark and your family's really close by.'

'I know.' His voice sounded as smooth as malt whisky and equally unperturbed.

'But don't you think it's a bit risk—?'

His mouth found her ear and it only took *one* delicious sweep of his tongue before her blood turned to melted chocolate and started spreading hot, sweet wonder through her. Before she realised what was happening, he'd pulled her back against him, wrapping his arms around her, and he was running his hand gently over her belly. Caressing her. Caressing the baby.

God, it felt so good that she wanted to stay resting against him for ever.

It can't feel good.

The defensive thought slammed into her and she froze as his hands changed from a caress to more of a palpating feel as if he was a doctor examining a patient. She brought her hands up onto his and in the process found her voice. 'What are you doing?'

'Just checking out Widget. You're bigger so I think he's grown.' He turned her in his arms. 'See? All that rest and good food is paying off.'

She tried to read his expression in the gloom cast by the canopy of the tree. 'I...I'm surprised you noticed.'

He laughed as if she was slightly slow and kissed her on the nose. 'Of course I noticed.' He stared at her for a long moment, twisting some of her hair around his fingers. 'George, who's going to be with you when you're in labour?'

I don't want blow-by-blow accounts about the pregnancy. Stunned, she almost asked, *Why?* 'Um...I've organised a doula through the birth centre. She came to all the classes with me.'

A horrified expression streaked across his face. 'You're paying someone?'

She tried to slough off his disapproval with the facts. 'My mother isn't here and I don't have a sister so this is the best solution.'

'But you'll be alone.'

She refused to let him make her feel bad. He had no clue what it was like to be without family. 'No, I'll have Joy.'

He paused, his mouth taking on a determined line. 'I want to be there.'

'Excuse me?' Surely she hadn't heard him say those words?

He swallowed hard, his blue-on-blue eyes catching hers. 'I want to be there for the birth of the baby.'

'But I… You don't…' Her brain seized, unable to process the words that were so at odds with everything he'd ever said. She dragged in a deep breath. 'We both decided that you're the donor. You've been adamant from the very start that you don't want anything to do with the baby, and I—'

'Correction.' He leaned in and his reassuring scent spun around her, followed by the gentle touch of his finger under her chin. He tilted her head up until their eyes locked. 'I want very much to be involved with the baby.'

His touch sent warm and caring tingles down to her toes, making instant sense of all his thoughtful gestures and the hovering he'd been doing over the past few days. All the things she'd worked so hard to stay immune to, with limited success.

I want very much to be involved.

Her heart quivered. He wanted them to be a family, and the castle she'd built momentarily a few days ago rose up out of the mist of her mind on a bedrock of foundations. 'You do?'

He grinned at her like he'd just ridden the best wave of the day. 'Georgie, I'm so excited about being a father.'

His enthusiasm washed over her, catching her own and

pulling it out from where she'd always stored it under wraps when they'd been together. She kissed him. 'I'm excited too and also a tiny bit terrified after what Annie and Erin told me today.'

He laughed and hugged her before dropping a kiss on her baby bump. 'I know what you mean, but it's going to be great. I've been listening to the recording I made of his heartbeat and I just wish he was here already so I can start my life as a dad.' His voice vibrated with excitement and delight. 'A dad. I never thought I'd be saying that. The idea of fatherhood used to terrify me and, God knows, I've run from it long enough.'

She beamed up at him, happiness pouring out of every pore. For over a year she'd thought she was going to be doing this motherhood gig on her own. She'd convinced herself she *had* to do it on her own and now her best friend, the man she loved—

Loved? Yes, loved. Now she could finally admit it to herself without being scared of rejection. She loved him totally and utterly, and way more than the love of a best friend.

You've loved him for years.

The truth was suddenly crystal clear. It was why she'd asked him to be the donor. Only now she could no longer think of him as a sperm donor. He was the father of her baby. *Their baby.*

Suddenly, the world was a magical, wonderful place and they were going to be parents and face the challenge together. All her anxieties about becoming a mother vanished and she wrapped her arms around his neck, needing to touch him and feel his reassuring strength. 'What made you change your mind?'

He shrugged. 'A few things. Being here on an extended visit with my nephews helped. I used to avoid long visits with the kids because of memories of Aaron. This year, the way Rupe looks at me reminds me of all the good times I spent with Aaron. Talking about him to you the other night really helped.'

'I'm glad.' She hugged to herself how special it made her feel that she was the only adult friend to whom he'd ever told the story of Aaron. 'So, parenthood...'

'Yeah.' His face spilt into a wide grin. 'Becoming a dad is going to be the most amazing experience of my life. I'm so ready for this. Ben's right—'

'Ben?' She checked because, more often than not, Hamish railed against the protestations of his eldest brother.

'Yeah.' He nodded enthusiastically. 'He told me I'd been trying fatherhood on for size this holiday and he made me realise it's exactly what I want.'

I thought I'd done that. An insidious chill made her shiver and she dropped her arms from his neck so she could think. 'How did Ben make you realise you want to be a dad?'

He glanced down, resting his hand on the under-curve of her belly, and a special smile she'd never seen before tugged at his lips. 'Ben and Caleb were talking about when Annie and Erin were pregnant, and how it made each of them feel almost primal about having created a child.'

Something about the way he said the words had her licking suddenly dry lips with a parched tongue. 'Do you...feel like that?'

'I do.' He pulled her back into his arms, his voice seductively low as he kissed her neck. 'They also said the sex was amazing and we both know all about that, don't we?'

She heard his voice in her head saying, *You pregnant... you're stunningly sexy and I want you.* It was immediately followed by the memory of his expression when she'd said, *Once I've had the baby and go back to my pre-pregnant size and shape, you'll no longer feel that way.*

Goose-bumps rose on her arms and her breath came in jerky waves. Not once in this conversation had he said he wanted her. All of it had been about him and the baby. His fatherhood dream. Her throat spasmed, making it hard to breathe.

He wants the baby; he doesn't want me.

Like the blasting force of gunpowder against rock, the foundations of her castle of dreams shattered into a thousand irreparable pieces. No man had ever truly wanted her. She'd always been convenient up to a point and then both Jonas and Luke had discarded her when she'd no longer been needed. Now it was happening again, only this time it was ten thousand times worse because it was her best friend, the man she truly loved, and for a few precious moments she'd hoped and dared to let her dreams soar.

Only dreams weren't real. Her life, however, was very, very real and she was back to where she'd started. This was *her* baby. Hers alone, and she had the paperwork to prove it. She would not be used as a convenient incubator and then discarded. She wouldn't allow that to happen and this time she was taking control. Squaring her shoulders, she took his hands off her hips and took a step backwards. 'Exactly where do I fit in with your fatherhood plans?'

Hamish had been deliciously distracted exploring the soft skin at the top of Georgie's shoulder when she'd jerked away from him, and as a result he hadn't really heard her question. 'Sorry?'

Her soft brown eyes had deepened to the colour of toffee and held a brittle edge. 'Right now I'm fecund with a baby and you think I'm incredibly sexy. Only this baby isn't something we created out of an overwhelming attraction, is it? Up until a week ago, when you saw me pregnant, I'd never been your type and the moment I've delivered the baby I'll go back to being the asexual woman I've always been to you.'

He blinked at her, completely stunned. If she'd given him an open-palmed slap to the cheek he couldn't have been more shocked. 'That's not true. I—'

'Really?' Her hands hit her hips as her brows hit her hairline. 'Who have you ever dated that wasn't ridiculously thin?'

He had no clue why she was even asking but he tried to oblige and think who'd had curves. The problem was all other women he'd dated had faded now his mind was deliciously full of Georgie. He came up blank.

'Exactly.'

'Georgie.' He tried to close the gap she'd put between them, wanting to tell her none of that mattered now. 'I don't care about how big you are.'

The moment the words left his mouth it was as if he heard the squeal of tyres and the unforgiving sound of a truck hitting a brick wall. *You're a moron.* He back-pedalled fast. 'That's not what I meant and you know it. Can we *please* go back to the bit where we're both excited about the baby?' With an imploring smile he reached for her hands.

She crossed her arms under her breasts. 'I don't think so.'

The stony look in her eyes rocked him and he suddenly felt more vulnerable than when he'd been under mortar attack in Africa. 'Why not?'

'It's not your baby.'

Was this what people meant by pregnancy hormones making women crazy? Because she wasn't making any sense. 'Of course it's my baby.'

She shook her head so hard her hair swung around her face, the softness of the strands contrasting with the sudden hard planes of her cheeks. 'No, it isn't. It's mine.'

White pain burned under his ribs.

'Hamish, we agreed that you wouldn't be involved with the baby and you can't just change your mind because you've decided you're ready to move on with your life and you want to try fatherhood on for size.'

His pain changed into the shape of anger. 'This isn't a whim, Georgie. I truly want this and I'm ready.'

Her mouth took on a grim line. 'Tough. You gave your rights away when you signed the donor papers.'

He'd never seen this side of her before and he didn't like it or understand it, but he knew enough to know that arguing his legal rights wasn't the way to sort out whatever it was that was eating at her. He tried the truth. 'George, we're best friends and we're having a baby together. I want to share all that.'

She flinched as if he'd struck her. 'And what did you have in mind?'

'I… We…' He ran his hand through his hair again, realising that he'd been so excited about the baby and telling her how he felt that he hadn't really thought much past that. He shot her what he hoped was an encouraging smile. 'We'll work it out as we go along. The important thing is—'

'How do you plan to parent when you're overseas three to six months of every year?'

'Obviously that will need some tweaking, but if you move into my place we—'

Her eyes narrowed to cold, hard slits. 'You think that the baby and I should move in and live with a man who's never had a relationship that lasted even six months?'

The vitriol in her voice shocked him as much as it scraped against his own barely leashed anger and bewilderment. 'You're exaggerating. Natasha and I were together for six months.'

She shook her head. 'Five and a half.'

'Lucy, then.'

She held up her hand, fingers splayed. 'Five.'

Incredulity swamped him. 'You have a mental catalogue of every woman I've ever dated?'

She gave a silent shrug.

'Georgie, the past is the past and it's over. I promise you, I'm ready to be a father.'

A flash of feeling he couldn't read burned in her eyes before fading fast. 'We're *friends*, Hamish, not a *couple*.'

'We're *more* than a couple, Georgie. We're about to be parents.'

Her nostrils flared. 'Exactly, and I'm not risking you calling it quits within six months, abandoning us and taking out our friendship with it. I really doubt you're ready to be a father, Hamish. I can't believe you've discarded years of not wanting to be responsible for another person in a mere three days and I'm sticking to the original plan. I'm having *my* baby and the birth certificate will not name the father.'

Like a knife to the heart, he bled. He'd thought she'd be thrilled with the idea of them becoming a family. Hell, for years, all she'd ever talked about had been settling down and combining her work with a family. He'd just offered her all of that, and she stood in front of him as if she could barely stand to be in his presence, while throwing all his hopes and dreams back in his face.

The irony hit him hard. After finally sharing the only secret he'd held back from her over all these years, and having her help him see that he was up for the challenge of being a father, she was now telling him he wasn't ready and that he had no chance to be involved.

Like hell he had no chance. He was done with being conciliatory and done with being nice. 'Georgina, I'm not ever going to have the chance to take out our friendship because you've just destroyed it. Utterly and irrevocably.'

Her throat worked as if she was trying hard not to cry but he didn't care. She'd just inflicted more pain on him than anyone ever had in his life, and his crushed heart formed a hard shell. 'I *will* be a father to this baby. You'll be hearing from my lawyer.'

Her chin lifted. 'And you'll be hearing from mine. Goodbye, Hamish.'

He gave her a curt nod and watched her walk away from

him in the fading light, leaving him surrounded by the detritus of what should have been the start of something wonderful.

Georgie stuffed the bare basics into her daypack, her tears dampening everything she touched. She bypassed most of her clothes, leaving them hanging in the wardrobe, and relegated the logistics of retrieving them to another time. Right now every cell in her body clamoured for her to leave. Leave Weeroona, Hamish and all the Pettigrews as fast as possible.

Beyond that, she had no plans and no clue where she'd spend the night. She'd sleep in her car if necessary, as long as it wasn't here.

Phone. Purse. Keys. She ran through her automatic check list. With everything ready, she sent up a quick hope that she wouldn't meet anyone on the stairs or in the foyer because she wasn't up to giving a coherent explanation about why she was leaving. Not without bursting into tears. As she gripped the large door handle, she paused for a moment, rubbing the ache in her lower back. 'Come on, Widget,' she urged. 'I need you to move into a more comfortable position just for the next few hours so I can drive to Melbourne.'

The baby didn't move. With a sigh she made her way downstairs. She was within three steps of the front door when she heard, 'Georgina?'

She bit her lip and turned, trying to plaster a normal smile on her face. 'Hi, Denise.'

Hamish's mother stared at the strap of the daypack, which was a stark black line against the white blouse Georgie had pulled on after discarding the plum pudding costume. Her gaze then fell to the car keys in Georgie's hand. 'Is everything all right?'

No, everything's a nightmare. Except for the baby, I've lost everything in my life I held dear. 'The party was wonderful, Denise. I hope you don't mind but...' her mind raced for a plausible excuse '… I just got a call from one of my practice colleagues. They've rented a house in Lorne and invited me for drinks.'

'Oh?' The inflection in Denise's voice said, *At this hour?* 'You look a bit pale to be driving. Why not take Hamish with you? I'm sure your friends would understand.'

She couldn't risk talking about Hamish so she shook her head and said, 'I'll stay the night. Goodbye, Denise.' Tears threatened to spill and knowing this was the last time she'd see Denise, she leaned in and kissed the cheek of a woman who'd been like a mother to her. 'Thanks for caring.'

She rushed through the door and out to her car before Denise could say another word. Adjusting her seat, she tried to find a way to sit where she didn't feel like the baby was pressing on her bladder or her stomach and her spine, but it didn't seem to make much difference. She wished she had two extra centimetres of room.

The drive down the winding road to Jindi took all her concentration and she had to work hard against the over-whelming feeling to plant her foot on the accelerator and speed away. As she drove past the 'Farewell Jindi River, come back soon' sign, her tears started anew, blurring her vision so badly that she pulled over. Fumbling with the glovebox catch, she finally found a box of tissues.

You've destroyed our friendship. Utterly and irrevocably. Hamish's words had been playing over and over in her head from the moment she'd walked away from him, digging deep and leaving scars.

She blew her nose and wiped her eyes. Hamish was the one who'd destroyed the friendship. He was the one who'd changed all the goalposts, wanting the baby and not wanting her, and leaving her completely bereft.

Yes, but you were the one who wanted more. Is it fair to cut him out of his child's life just because he doesn't love you the way you want to be loved?

Her belly tightened as the baby did a huge roll.

She touched the rigid muscles. 'What's your opinion, Widget? Did I destroy it? Am I to blame?'

A large pop sounded and fluid gushed between her legs. She gave a wobbly laugh, not quite able to believe her waters had just broken. 'Okay. No need to panic,' she said out loud to the silent night, trying to reassure herself as excitement ran parallel to tempered alarm. 'Waters broken, first labour and no contractions. It would be nicer if I had a towel.'

She knew from her obstetric rotation as a medical student and from her prenatal classes that it could be hours before she went into true labour, which left her time to drive to Melbourne. 'Looks like we have a bed for the night after all, Widget.'

Picking up her phone, she brought up the number of the labour ward at the Royal Women's Hospital and moved her thumb to press the call button when a massive wave of pain hit her.

Gasping, she dropped the phone and gripped the steering-wheel, trying to remember how to breathe and go with the contraction when every part of her wanted to clench tight and hard against it. It seemed to go on for ever but finally it faded and she fell back against the seat, dripping in sweat.

She glanced at the green light of the car clock. Ten twenty-five. First labours generally started with fifteen minutes between contractions or even longer. She supposed she could drive in fifteen—

Another contraction ripped into her, stronger and longer than the previous one, and she gasped as the full impact hit her. This wasn't a drill, this was the real deal and there was no turning back. She was in labour and soon she'd be a mother. Excitement and fear hit head on and the moment the contraction finished, she grabbed her phone and pressed 000.

* * *

'Okay, so now I'm convinced something is going on,' Denise said as she walked into the kitchen.

Hamish, who was elbow-deep in suds, didn't look up. 'Can't I help out without you thinking there's some ulterior motive?'

Denise moved in next to him, tea-towel in hand. 'The year after Aaron died, your father scrubbed more pots and chopped more wood than he's ever done since.'

'It's too dark to chop wood.'

'It's too late for Georgina to be visiting friends in Lorne, especially when her usually happy eyes are red-rimmed from crying.'

Guilt that he'd made Georgie cry had his hands stalling on the greasy pan. *She's the one who rejected me.* His fingers vigorously recommenced scrubbing.

His mother's hand touched his shoulder. 'You and Georgina, you're more than just good friends, aren't you?'

His anger, which had burned so hot and bright for an hour, dimmed slightly as sadness sneaked in. 'We're not even friends now.'

'I think that's probably an exaggeration,' Denise said, resuming drying. 'It would take something huge to destroy a solid seventeen-year friendship.'

He met his mother's concerned gaze. More than anything he wanted to tell her about Georgie and the baby, but now it was all such a tangled and complex situation it would only bring her heartache. It was destroying him. 'Yeah, it would.'

'Hamish!' His father's voice yelled out a moment before he appeared in the doorway, confusion and dismay on his face. 'There you are. I just got a call from Lexie Daniels, the nurse on duty at the hospital. Georgina's there and in labour.'

Hamish dropped the saucepan into the sink, sending suds airborne. 'What?'

Roy shook his head, sharing his shock. 'I don't understand either. Why didn't she tell any of us or at least ask us to drive her? But all that aside, she's at the hospital and—'

'I'm on my way.' Hamish dried his hands on his shorts.

Roy shook his head. 'Sorry, Hamish, but Lexie said Georgina was adamant she didn't want you there.'

CHAPTER TWELVE

HAMISH swayed and gripped the sink as a barrage of emotions thundered through him, leaving behind a bleeding wound and fulminating anger. He hadn't thought it was possible for Georgie to hurt him any more tonight, but he'd been wrong. His father's words punched him hard in the gut, reminding him of exactly how emotionally incapable she thought him and how determined she was to keep him from his child.

'If she doesn't want me there then why on earth did Lexie bother ringing?'

'She's on duty alone and our doctor's at a Christmas function at Apollo Bay. Lexie wants you there as back-up should there be a problem.' His father gave him an apologetic look. 'Perhaps your mother should go and be the support for Georgina.'

'No!' The word roared out of him. Damn it, why was Georgie doing this? Why was she locking him out of her life? It made no sense. Hell, they'd always been each other's safety nets. Their baby was about to be born and they should be together, sharing this.

Georgie had always been there for him when he'd needed her and despite what she'd said to him tonight, he wanted to be there for her. He needed to do this for her. No woman should go through labour alone.

He picked up his keys. 'I don't care what Georgie says.

No matter what she thinks or how crazy she's been acting tonight, she's not always right, and I'm not letting the woman I love go through labour without me.'

His parents stared at him for a moment before exchanging one of their secret looks and then Denise said, 'Hamish, does Georgie know you love her?'

The question slammed into him, jolting him hard. He opened his mouth to say *yes*, only to shut it again. Surely she knew. After all, she'd thrown it back in his face two hours ago. He could picture her in his mind's eye—her flinch of pain when he'd said, '*Georgie we're best friends and we're having a baby together. I want to share all that.*'

She'd recoiled from him as if he'd been the one to wound her when she'd been the one to inflict the deepest cut of all, denying him any involvement with the baby. It still floored him that she'd said it because she'd always wanted the whole white-picket-fence, family experience.

Her words from a year ago echoed in his head. *I'm having this baby on my own so there's no risk of me and the baby being abandoned when a man decides yet again that I'm not enough for him.*

His stomach plummeted. Oh, God, Georgie didn't know he loved her. How stupid could he possibly have been? He'd failed to say the words *I love you* to a woman who'd been hurt and left twice before. All she'd known was that he wanted to be a father and she thought that meant he didn't want her. He'd been so excited and carried away about the baby, so full of the joy of them being parents together and spending the rest of their lives together, that he'd assumed she'd known what he'd meant.

He was a class-A fool. His keys dug into his palm but he didn't care. All he knew was that he had to get to the hospital right now.

'Hamish,' his mother said, her eyes suddenly filled with questions, 'is the—?'

'I'll ring you when I have news,' Hamish said quickly, striding to the door. No way was he admitting to anything until he'd told Georgie he loved her. More importantly, until he'd found a way for her to believe him.

The half-marathon Georgie had once run was a walk in the park compared to labour. She'd never worked so hard in her life. As each contraction started, she gripped the mask, gulping in nitrous oxide so its effects hit just before the peak of the contraction levelled her. It didn't feel like it was doing all that much, but holding the mask and focussing on her breathing helped. At least, that was what she was telling herself.

The contraction passed and she rolled off all fours and sank back onto the bank of cushions on the floor. The squeak of the door opening made her look up. Lexie had left the room when the night bell had pealed, leaving Georgie alone to face two contractions without the nurse's calming voice.

'Sorry about that. I had to give Carolyn a quick handover,' Lexie said with a distracted smile.

Georgie couldn't stop the sob of relief from escaping from her throat. 'I'm glad you're back. It's such—' The contraction stole the rest of her sentence.

'Hard work.' Lexie wiped Georgie's brow with a damp cloth as the contraction eased. 'I know it is, but it's all worth it when you hold your baby in your arms.' She offered Georgie a drink. 'As well as Carolyn arriving to look after the other two patients, Dr Pettigrew is here. He's waiting outside.'

Of course he is. She wanted to bang her head against something really hard. It was bad enough she'd gone into labour in Jindi River without her support person or any baby clothes, but now the universe was taunting her with the presence of the one person she didn't want anywhere near her.

Lexie had the grace to look slightly contrite. 'I know you're saying that you don't want anyone with you, but I know you've been staying with the Pettigrews and as things progress you might change your mind.'

Betrayal burned through her. 'I won't.'

Lexie smiled at her as if she was privy to a secret that Georgie wasn't in on. The one thing Georgie was certain about was that the only reason Hamish had come to the hospital was because he wanted to be here for the birth of his baby.

My baby. It's my baby.

Her convictions weren't loud enough to drown out the memory of his angry and hurt voice, which refused to be silenced. As she rode the next contraction, she kept hearing his words, *'You'll be hearing from my lawyer. I will be a father to this baby.'*

The pain trailed off and she sank back again into the pillows, remembering exactly how his face had looked when he'd said that—hard with fury, and his eyes chilly ice-blue and filled with bitter intent. She believed without a doubt Hamish would be taking her to court and yet he hadn't marched into the labour ward, insisting on his rights as a father. He was *waiting* outside.

Waiting for permission from her to enter? She closed her eyes, putting Hamish in the 'too-hard basket' of her life. Right now she didn't have the energy to cope with him. Her focus needed to be on her labour and her baby, but despite telling herself that she said, 'Did he ask to come in?'

'No. All he said was that he was here if you needed him.' Lexie was busy palpating her abdomen, finding the lie of the baby, and a moment later the sonograph blared out the rapid heartbeat. 'Sounds perfect.' She wiped away the gel and gave her an unhappy look. 'Georgina, the birth of a baby is a once-in-a-lifetime experience. Are you absolutely certain there isn't anyone you want me to call to be here with you for the birth, because regret can eat at you for a long time.'

She heard the words, felt them even, although she would have done anything to block them out.

Punishing Hamish by denying him access to the baby just because he doesn't love you isn't love.

You don't want him here, her head overruled her heart.

Another contraction rocked her, the intensity so much stronger than all previous contractions. It seared her with burning fire, stealing her breath, sucking her down into a deep black pit and pushing her way beyond the brink of control.

'Hamish!'

She heard his name and was shocked to realise she'd been the one screaming it.

The door opened instantly and he strode in, his face taut with worry. He fell to his knees and caught her hand in his. 'I'm here, Georgie. I'm right here.'

His hair stood up on end, his curls chaotic and rumpled as if he'd raked his hands through them a thousand times. The edges of his eyes and mouth were tight with strain and he looked completely stressed-out and gorgeous. She loved him so much that her heart wept.

He doesn't love you, just the baby.

Another contraction hit and the tunnel of pain engulfed her again, surrounding her in a ring of fire. She gasped for breath. 'I hate you, Hamish Pettigrew,' she sobbed, and moaned, pushing his hands away. 'I really, really hate you.'

'That's just transition talking,' Lexie said mildly as she checked the delivery pack and added gloves.

'I'm not so sure it is, Lex.' Hamish sounded desperately sad as he put down the drink bottle he'd just pressed to Georgie's lips. He linked his fingers through hers. 'Georgie, I love you. I really love you. I know my timing's lousy and I should have told you sooner, and I hate it that I didn't but— Ouch!'

She hadn't realised it but she'd sunk her nails into his hand as the next contraction crushed her, making her shake uncontrollably, fuzzing her brain and making her hear voices.

She'd just imagined Hamish telling her he loved her, which she knew was only wishful thinking. Had he really said that he loved her, not just the baby, but her too? 'I hate this. I can't do it any more, it's all too hard.' Tears streamed down her face as all her plans for her labour and her life spun out of control.

I want to go home,' she tried to say, but it came out on a low grunt. 'But I don't have one.'

'George,' Hamish said quietly but firmly, and his fingers lightly gripped her chin, 'look at me. You have a home and your baby's coming now. Nothing's going to stop it.'

Gulping in air and crying at the same time, she stared up at him and into his amazing and hypnotic eyes. Like a wave rolling back off the sand, her panic receded, leaving behind a focussed calm. The baby's head pressed down, giving her a full and urgent sensation. 'Haim, I want to push.'

'Great.' He nodded, his expression encouraging. 'With your next contraction, bear down.'

And she did.

Contraction after contraction she pushed, gripping Hamish's hand, holding on fast as if she thought he might suddenly disappear. With each contraction his strong arms helped her move forward and he quietly coached her, and when the contraction ended he gently eased her back onto the cushions, gave her water and fanned her sweating body.

'I see a head,' Lexie said finally. 'Next contraction, Georgina, I need you to pant when I tell you.'

'I'm so tired.' Exhaustion ran through her veins like treacle. 'I can't even think.'

Hamish cooled her face with a damp cloth. 'You're doing an amazing job, Georgie. I'm in awe of your stamina.'

She gave him a tired smile. 'I'm almost out— Ohh…'

She didn't think she could possibly find the energy to push any more but her body had different plans.

'Pant, Georgina.'

'Can't,' she grunted.

'Pant with me, George.' Hamish's breath sounded in her ear and she struggled to match it. Suddenly the burning fire eased and pressure changed.

'Your baby's head is born,' Lexie said with a smile, 'and he's rotating perfectly.'

Hamish rubbed her shoulder. 'Nearly there. You're acing this.'

She didn't feel very ace. She just wanted it over.

'Georgina,' Lexie said, 'make this contraction count.'

'What, and the other's haven't?' Her belly tightened with the now-familiar bands of steel. 'Now.'

'You can do this, George, you're a natural.' Hamish's arms supported her and with his encouragement flowing through her she gave it everything she had.

'Top shoulder out…' Lexie reported. 'Bottom shoulder out and…'

A wet and slippery body was laid on Georgie's belly and she sank back in relief and wonder as she gazed at her beautiful baby. 'Hello.'

Enormous dark blue eyes stared at her in quiet contemplation as if to say, *I know* you.

Crying, she caressed the wet head, in awe of her baby's existence, and then exhaustion claimed her, turning her utterly limp. She heard the snip of scissors as Lexie cut the cord and the jab of a needle in her thigh as her body continued to tremble so hard she was desperately worried she'd drop the baby.

She bit her lip and looked at Hamish, whose eyes had filled with tears. 'I can't stop shaking. Can you hold him, examine him, tell me he's all right?'

'Are you sure?'

His earnest look brought new tears and she didn't understand why. Somehow she managed to nod.

He pressed a kiss to her forehead then scooped up the baby in a towel and took him over to the receiving cot.

'Okay, Georgie, any urges to push the placenta out?' Lexie palpated her now soggy belly.

The thought of having to push anything out of herself ever again was almost too much to contemplate but within a few minutes she did. Lexie helped her up onto the bed, propping her still-trembling body with a stack of pillows. 'Why can't I stop shaking?'

'Precipitate labour. From your waters breaking to delivery was three and a half hours, which is incredibly quick, and your body's in a bit of shock. It's unlikely to last longer than an hour.' Lexie tucked the sheet around her. 'Come on, Hamish, Georgina needs her baby and a full report. I'll leave you to it.'

As Lexie left the room, Georgie turned her head, watching Hamish walk toward her with a smile she imagined was replicated on her own face. 'Is he okay? Lungs clear, no heart murmur?'

'Georgie, she's perfect.'

Hamish watched the shocked surprise wash over Georgie's pale but beautiful face and felt his own tears fall.

Her mouth opened and for a moment no sound came out. 'She? She's a girl? But…' Joy and bewilderment danced on her cheeks.

'Yeah, I know,' he said softly as he laid his miracle daughter—the first Pettigrew girl born to his branch of the family in five generations—onto the bed next to Georgie. He'd had seven precious minutes to study her from top to toe, to imprint her on his memory—her soft fontenelle, her button nose and the way her long, long fingers with their tiny pearl nails formed a vice-like grip on his forefinger.

He was a doctor and he knew that all healthy babies did this, but when she'd wrapped her fingers around his, she'd also wrapped them around his heart. He was a father and his first job was to tell her mother how much he loved them both.

Georgie gazed down at her daughter. For years she'd been dreaming of becoming a mother and for the past eight and a half months she'd known this day was coming, but now it was here, it had an unreal quality to it. She curved her hand around the top of her daughter's head, feeling her warmth and the reassurance that she did actually exist.

Hamish swung out a chair and sat down, leaning his arms on the bed with the baby between them. It wasn't lost on Georgie that the baby wasn't the only thing between them— so were the unresolved issues around the baby and the fact he'd just witnessed her in the most vulnerable moments of her life.

'Thank you for letting me be here for her birth.' His eyes scanned her face. 'I wasn't certain you'd want me.'

'I wasn't either.' She swallowed hard against the tears that threatened to bubble up again. God, she hadn't known childbirth made you so weepy. 'I didn't think I did, but thanks for guiding me through the tough bits.'

Anguish filled his face. 'Georgie, about earlier tonight…'

No, not now. 'I've just had a baby, Hamish, and I can't do this right now.' She blinked fast as she gazed at her little girl, feeling the tug of a love so strong that it bound her to her soul. Right then she knew that if Hamish even felt a tenth of that love for his daughter then she couldn't deny him the right to be part of her life, even if every access visit and phone call would remind her of how much she loved him and how devastating it was that he couldn't reciprocate.

'I know you want to be an active father and I promise you that we'll come to some sort of an arrangement. Weekends, something. We'll talk in a few weeks.'

'I don't want that, Georgie.'

'Be fair, Hamish. You've always been fair and right now

it's all I can offer.' Her voice broke and a tear splashed on the baby's face, making her eyes open in surprise.

'Georgie, my George.' His voice wavered over her name in a way it never had before. 'I love you. I want to be with you every single day.'

She shook her head, knowing what he said wasn't true. 'You love the baby and now you think you love me, but you don't.'

'Yes. I do.' His firm voice was quiet, calm but absolutely determined.

She chewed her thumbnail. 'You're letting the life-altering feelings of seeing your child born get in the way of what's real.'

'No. I'm not.'

The intensity of his gaze gave gravitas to his words. *You're killing me, Haim.* 'In seventeen years you've never loved me so why would I believe you now? I'm the mother of your child but I won't have you using me as a convenience.' Her voice broke. 'I deserve to be loved.'

He wrung his hands. 'Georgie, believe me, you are loved. I think I've loved you for years, only I didn't know. Call me stupid, because I am.' He ran his hands through his hair.

'I know I made a total mess of things tonight at the party by assuming you knew I loved you and by not actually saying the words. I'd do anything to turn back time and start over. I'll do anything to make you believe me when I say you are the woman I love and the woman of my heart. I won't ever, ever leave you. I love you, Georgie.'

The words she would have welcomed four short hours ago fell like stones, bruising her heart. 'How can I trust you not to leave me like everyone else?'

He slid his hand over hers, letting it rest there with only the pressure of its natural weight. 'Have I ever left you?'

She sighed in frustration. 'Hamish, we've never even dated, let alone been in a relationship.'

'Have I ever left you? Think about it, Georgie.' His eyes implored her to do as he asked. 'When your parents died, I was there for you. Through the punishing years of med school and residency, I was there for you, just like you were for me. Even through your break-ups, when you needed me I was there or at least I was on the end of a scratchy phone line.'

A smile broke the serious line of his mouth. 'Hey, I've even accompanied you to weddings when you said you didn't want to take a date because you wanted to relax, enjoy and be yourself. You do that with *me*.'

His words caressed her but she couldn't afford to let them. 'That's because we were friends.'

His thumb softly stroked the back of her hand. 'We're way more than friends. We fit together like two halves of a whole and we always have done. Outside my family, you're the most constant person in my life. I always want to tell you my news first and thoughts of you have got me through some tough times overseas.'

She heard his love for her in his voice and saw it on his face, and her heart turned over. He was right. He'd never left her, ever. For seventeen years he'd always been there for her in some shape or form. He'd even helped her get pregnant when the thought of fatherhood had terrified him.

He'd never left her and he never would.

Amazement and joy rushed through her. 'You really do love me?'

His mouth wobbled with emotion and he brought her hand to his lips and kissed it before sucking in a deep breath. 'I really, really do.'

He really, really did. Now she wanted to know more. 'When did you realise you loved me?'

He laced the fingers of one hand through hers. 'Consciously? At six-seventeen tonight, when the thought of being with you and becoming a father filled me with joy and I could picture us growing old together. At eight-fifty when you broke my heart by telling me I couldn't be part of your life.'

'Sorry.'

He shook his head. 'No, it was my fault and from now on I'm telling you that I love you every day. Georgie, now I know what love is, I can honestly tell you I've always loved you. It's probably why none of my relationships have lasted longer than six months.'

'Five and half,' she teased, as a blissful freedom blew through her. Now she knew he loved her she realised it was time to tell him exactly how she felt. 'Hamish, I've loved you for years, but we wanted such different things out of life I accepted we didn't have that sort of future together. Please know that when I asked you to help me have our daughter I had no expectation that we would end up together. It wasn't planned.'

'I know, but thank God you asked or I might never have realised what I've been missing out on all these years.' He tickled the baby's feet and then looked up at her. 'I love you, Georgina Harriet Lambert. You're smart, funny, sexy, my best friend and now you've given me the most amazing gift of a daughter. I want to spend the rest of my life with you, starting right this second. Will you marry me?'

She didn't know it was possible to be this happy and the tears flowed again. 'I love you so much, Hamish James Pettigrew.'

'Yes, but will you marry me?' His expression had a slight tinge of worry to it.

She cupped his cheek. 'Name the day and I'll be there.'

He leaned in and his lips covered her mouth with love and such caring that her heart overflowed with a happiness she hadn't known was possible.

The baby gave her first real cry and Georgie picked her up, snuggling her to her chest. 'And I love you too, our yet-to-be-named baby.'

Hamish helped Georgie attach their daughter to the breast, loving it that he was able to share all of this with her and that the trauma of the past few hours was now a distant memory. 'Do you have any girls' names picked out?'

She raised her brows at him, a cheeky smile splitting her face. 'You told me she would be a boy.'

'Sorry about that.' He kissed her again and then gazed at them both while their daughter suckled gustily and noisily for a few minutes before falling asleep.

'Haim.'

'Yeah?'

'I think we need to phone your parents and tell them about their granddaughter.'

He agreed but he knew the moment he officially announced the birth of his daughter, the wonderful circus that was his family would descend on them, enveloping them in love, and this precious and wonderful quiet time together would vanish. 'Five more minutes?'

'I love them dearly, but I was thinking ten?'

He laughed, loving the synergy between them that he'd always taken for granted and had come far too close to losing. 'I love you, George.'

She smiled up at him with her soft eyes shining, and he knew he was home.

EPILOGUE

THE Jindi River Christmas Eve community carol service on the foreshore was in full swing. The attendance was bigger this year, thanks to the influx of Pettigrews, many of whom had stayed on to celebrate the birth of Virginia Natalie Pettigrew.

At three days old she was unfazed by all the fuss or the fact that her father was wearing a tea-towel on his head and her mother a long shapeless shift. Later in life she'd show a lot more interest in the gifts her uncles and grandfather had brought her, although no matter how much they teased her Daddy, she'd know that he was a very wise man. At least she would until she turned fifteen.

'Hey, 'Ginia,' Rupert leaned over the crib with a seriously disappointed look on his face. 'You can't be the baby Jesus 'cos you're a girl.'

Hamish laughed and tousled his hair. 'Mate, you're going to learn that girls can pretty much do what they want to do.'

He caught Georgie's gaze and shared a smile with her—one that was filled with a message that only the two of them could understand. 'In fact, Rupe, often girls can change your mind and get you to do things you never expected.'

The four-year-old gave his uncle a disgusted look. 'Baby girls are boring.'

'Right now she is but next Christmas, she'll be walking and wanting to play.'

Rupert absorbed that bit of information. 'I can teach her stuff.'

'You can and that will be wonderful.'

Roy and Denise strolled over arm in arm. 'How's our baby girl?' Denise said, cooing over her granddaughter.

'*My* daughter,' Hamish said, loving the rush of joy it gave him every time he spoke those two words, 'is a total star in her first Jindi Christmas pageant. Just like her mother.'

Georgie laughed, picking at her costume. 'When I'd dreamed of fame I was better dressed than this.'

He pulled her close and kissed her. 'You're beautiful.'

His parents exchanged one of their looks and Hamish grinned. 'I finally get what you two do with that silent messaging thing.'

Roy slapped him on the back. 'We're so thrilled you do because we'd almost given up. Still, even though it took you way too long, you've done good.'

He turned to Georgie as Denise moved in next to him. 'Denise and I are so thrilled you're part of our family, Georgina, and we're over the moon to have a granddaughter. We hope over time you'll come to think of us not just as the dreaded in-laws but as friends.'

Georgie surfed the wave of emotion that hit her, not wanting to cry again because everyone would just shake their head indulgently and say, 'she's just had a baby'. Sure, she had, and she had a tendency to tear up every time she gazed at Ginny or Hamish but this—this was different. From the moment she'd met Roy and Denise and they'd gathered her up into their caring lives, putting her into the heart of their family, she'd started to love them almost as much as she'd loved her mum and dad.

'Is it okay if I think of you as parents and friends?'

This time it was Roy and Denise who blinked rather quickly as they hugged her tightly.

'Have you thought about where you're going to live?' Denise asked, her voice straining to be casual.

Georgie glanced at Hamish, who nodded as if to say, *you tell them.* Two nights ago they'd sat up gazing at their sleeping daughter and had discussed all the logistics that went along with merging two households and two independent lives and becoming a family. 'We want Ginny to be close to her grandparents so I'm going to sell my house in Melbourne and we'll live in Geelong. There's a doctor shortage so I won't have any trouble finding work.'

Denise clapped her hands in delight.

'And I'm not going to be the team leader on quite so many Giving Back projects,' Hamish said. 'I don't want to miss out on seeing Ginny growing up.'

'But I want him to do one overseas trip a year.' Georgie squeezed his hand, reassuring him that she didn't want him to totally give up something he loved. 'A six-week stint, so when he's away I thought it might be nice to come down here on my days off and—'

'We'll be holding you to that,' Roy said with a wide smile.

Harry rushed over yelling, 'Nana! Da! It's time,' and the rest of the immediate family followed him, all wearing their nativity costumes.

'Come on, Pettigrews, everyone into position,' said Hamish as the MC took the microphone and announced it was time for everyone's favourite Christmas song. 'Ben, your tea-towel's crooked, Caleb, you're presenting the third gift after Dad and— Harry and Jack, stop teasing the sheep.'

'For a man who didn't have the foresight to book any accommodation for his pregnant girlfriend you're awfully bossy,' Erin said with a smile as she lifted Rupert, complete with angel wings, onto her shoulders.

'No cheek from the props, thank you,' Hamish said, his blue eyes dancing.

Georgie laughed, loving that she was part of this loud and giving family and that Ginny would grow up in the heart of it. As the band played the introduction to 'Away in a Manger', Hamish sat down next to her, slipping his arm around her, and pulling her in close. 'Ready?'

'For the rest of my life with you? Absolutely.'

He leaned in and kissed her. 'Merry Christmas, my darling Georgie.'

'Merry Christmas, Haim.'

And she knew this wonderful Christmas was only the first of many more and she couldn't wait.

* * * * *

A sneaky peek at next month...

Medical Romance

CAPTIVATING MEDICAL DRAMA—WITH HEART

My wish list for next month's titles...

In stores from 7th December 2012:

❑ From Christmas to Eternity – Caroline Anderson

& Her Little Spanish Secret – Laura Iding

❑ Christmas with Dr Delicious – Sue MacKay

& One Night That Changed Everything – Tina Beckett

❑ Christmas Where She Belongs – Meredith Webber

& His Bride in Paradise – Joanna Neil

Available at WHSmith, Tesco, Asda, Eason, Amazon and Apple

Just can't wait?

MILLS & BOON Book Club

2 Free Books!

Get your free books now at

www.millsandboon.co.uk/freebookoffer

Or fill in the form below and post it back to us

THE MILLS & BOON® BOOK CLUB™—HERE'S HOW IT WORKS: Accepting your free books places you under no obligation to buy anything. You may keep the books and return the despatch note marked 'Cancel'. If we do not hear from you, about a month later we'll send you 5 brand-new stories from the Medical™ series, including two 2-in-1 books priced at £5.49 each and a single book priced at £3.49*. There is no extra charge for post and packaging. You may cancel at any time, otherwise we will send you 5 stories a month which you may purchase or return to us—the choice is yours. *Terms and prices subject to change without notice. Offer valid in UK only. Applicants must be 18 or over. Offer expires 31st January 2013. **For full terms and conditions, please go to www.millsandboon.co.uk/freebookoffer**